Isabel Wyatt

King Beetle-Tamer

and other light-hearted
wonder tales

Floris Books

Illustrations by Astrid Maclean

First published by Dawne-Leigh Publications in 1980
This edition published in 1994 by Floris Books
Reprinted in 1997

British Library CIP Data available

ISBN 0-86315-526-X

Printed in Great Britain
by Page Bros (Norwich) Ltd

King Beetle-Tamer

Contents

King Beetle-Tamer

On the day Orfeo was born, his father died. A year later, as Orfeo lay asleep in the bog-oak cradle in his mother's kitchen, an old woman of the roads knocked at the door of the tumbledown cabin and begged for a bit of bread.

"Come in and rest your bones by the fire while you eat it," invited Orfeo's mother.

While the old woman rested her bones by the fire, she peered into the cradle at the sleeping child.

"Och, but he's a broth of a boy!" she wheezed. (For all this took place in Ireland.)

"Indeed and he is," agreed his mother, just like any mother.

"It is into a merry gossoon he will grow," said the old woman.

"Indeed and why not?" said his mother.

"He will die in his bed," said the old woman.

"We do in these parts," said his mother.

"But not young and not crushed by a falling wall," said the old woman, "as this one is like to do. But if he has the luck *not* to, he will be king after the king."

The summer Orfeo grew up into a merry gossoon (as long and lean as two yards of pump water), his mother turned him out of his box bed by the kitchen chimney wall and sent him to sleep out-of-doors, as far away from walls as he could get.

"It is for love of your life I do this, my pulse, my

treasure," she told him. "A fine mother I would be if I let a tumbling wall stop you being a king!"

Orfeo went out to sleep in the meadow without a murmur. But it worried him to think he might well commit a million murders each time he lay down in the grass. So before he lay down he stamped three times, to warn all the local insects and creeping things, and give them time to get safely away.

Away they all scuttled and scurried for dear life. But as soon as Orfeo was settled on his back, looking up at the evening star in the sunset sky, back they all came.

"He is as sweet as a long streak of honey," cried the lady creeping things, each standing on her six toes, the better to admire him. "And, look, his nose is all over ladybird freckles!"

"What is more to the point, he is kind," said their menfolk, each waving his two front legs to mark his words. "From now on, he is our mother and our father."

The creeping things told the field mice, and the field mice told the birds. When Orfeo woke at dawn, he had a levee fit for a French king, with the songbirds making chamber music, the butterflies fluttering about him, and all the little meadow creatures standing round and bowing their heads off like real courtiers.

All that summer, Orfeo slept out in the meadow. But with the fall of the leaves, his mother died; and as the nights grew longer and colder, he thought:

"While she was here, I did her will to save her worry. But she must surely know now that to run away from a danger is not the right way to meet it. What is to be will be, wherever I sleep."

So he came indoors and slept again in the box bed in the kitchen, snug and cosy against the warm chimney wall.

The night frosts came, nine white ones in a row, and then a black one which left the meadow burned up with its freezing fire. When Orfeo went out on the tenth morning, a piping voice rose from every ruined grass blade at his feet:

"O, Orfeo, you are our mother and our father. There is no longer shelter for us here. Will you give us leave to winter in the crannies of your walls?"

"With a heart and a half!" cried Orfeo.

And he held the kitchen door wide open for them.

In they flew, in they scuttled. Beetles' wing cases shut with a click, and shrews' tails vanished like bits of string, as they tucked themselves away in each crack and cranny. They tucked themselves away so well that at first Orfeo hardly knew they were there.

But as they grew more at home, they woke up now and then and crept out of their beds to keep him company. The crickets would sing on the hearth in the dusk when Orfeo sat by the fire. On days of winter sun, the butterflies hanging with folded wings in dark corners would flutter to his finger tip, to bask in the warmth. The mice would steal out from their holes in the wainscot and sit up to beg for crumbs, their whiskers twitching, their eyes as bright as beads.

Orfeo's neighbours came to him and said:

"Orfeo, winter is the best time to repair a shaky cabin, while there is less to do. Tell us when you are ready, and we will give you a hand."

Orfeo thanked them and said:

"Let us put it off till spring. I have winter guests; it would be a pity to disturb them."

The winter wore on. On February first, St Bridget's Day, the year quickened. At the first smell of spring on the way, Orfeo's winter guests woke wide awake and streamed out-of-doors again.

"*Now* I can put my house in order," said Orfeo.

But already the birds had begun to put on their courting colours, and to choose their sweethearts; and in only a fortnight came St Valentine's Day, when the birds get married.

Pair by pair they came now to Orfeo, and bowed to him with their wing tips on their hearts, and told him he was their mother and their father, and begged leave to build their nests on the outside of his cabin — the starlings in the thatch, the jackdaws in the chimney, the swallows under the eaves, the tomtits in the ivy, the robins in the crumbling niches in the wall.

"With a heart and a half!" cried Orfeo.

What a coming and going there was then, with beakfuls of sticks and straw and hay and mud and horsehair and everything else good for home-making! And when the nests were finished and furnished with eggs, with each mother bird keeping them warm with the live quilt of her own body, how that choir of proud fathers sang all over that tumbledown cabin!

Orfeo's neighbours came to him again, and said:

"Orfeo, that chimney wall will fall about your ears if you do not mend it, and soon we shall be far too busy to help you."

Orfeo thanked them and said:

"Let us put it off till summer. I have spring guests; it would be a pity to disturb them."

(Yes, even the jackdaw he did not want to disturb, though his nest in the chimney made the fire smoke dreadfully.)

The spring wore on. The eggs in each nest hatched. From dawn to dusk the parent birds flew to and fro, to and fro, filling the gaping mouths of their naked nestlings. Then the first feathers came; and still the parent birds flew to and fro, to and fro, teaching their fledglings to fly.

"As soon as the baby birds can fly," said Orfeo, "I can put my house in order."

But before the baby birds could fly, the hive bees began to swarm.

Now in those days only straw hives were used; the box hives of today, in which the bees can live year after year, had not yet been invented. When men took the honey from the straw hives once a year, they had first to stifle the bees with sulphur smoke. And one wise and wily old queen bee, when it came to her turn that year to lead out a new colony, made up her mind to save them from this fate.

So, leaving the parent hive one warm May morning, with her worker bees streaming behind her, she made a beeline to Orfeo and settled on his nose. The first worker bees clung to her, and more worker bees streaming behind her, till a ball of bees, like a rich, brown, seething plum pudding, was hanging from Orfeo's nose tip.

"O, Orfeo, you are our mother and our father," piped the queen bee from the middle of this mass. "Give us leave to make our new home in your rafters."

"With a heart and a half!" cried Orfeo fervently.

So into Orfeo's kitchen streamed the bees, and at once were as busy as bees can be in its rafters. Soon there were white, gleaming combs of six-sided cells hanging from the thick black beams, and in some of the cells the queen was laying eggs for all she was worth, while in others golden honey and bee-bread were being stored as fast as the nectar and pollen they were made from were brought in from the flowers.

"Now I *can't* set my house in order," said Orfeo to himself, "for *these* guests will be with me the whole year through."

So winter came round again. The insects came indoors again to shelter in cracks and crannies; the field mice came back to their mouse-holes; the crickets sang again on the hearth. Those birds who had not flocked south for the winter came back to their old family homes in thatch and wall and ivy, and the sparrows moved into the swallows' empty houses under the eaves. The bees' humming among the rafters had stopped; the workers clung to the queen in a sleeping ball.

The winter storms set in. The winter winds roared and howled round the chimney. But Orfeo slept snug and sound in his warm bed; and all his two-legged, four-legged and six-legged guests slept snug and sound in theirs.

Then a night came when the quiet kitchen, lit dimly by the stable lantern hung beside the door, was invaded by every insect and creeping thing that had been tucked up in the cracks and crannies of the chimney wall, while out of its mouse-holes scuttled generations of mice, from bald old great-grandfathers to frisky babes with the bloom still on their fur.

They swarmed over the sleeping Orfeo. They tickled his face, the insects with their feet, the mice with their whiskers; and as soon as they felt his eyelids flutter, they chanted all together:

"O, Orfeo, you are our mother and our father. Give us leave to inform you that the wind has broken the chimney wall's back, and it is about to fall."

In one bound, Orfeo was out of his bed. In a wave of mice and insects, a blast of wind blew him to the other side of the room. There was a crash and a roar; the air was thick with dust. As it cleared, Orfeo saw a great, jagged gap in the chimney wall; and below it, under a heap of stones and rubble, his bed was smashed to smithereens.

Through the hole in the wall the chimney jackdaw came flying. He began to beat with his wings at the fallen stones, to scrabble at them with beak and claws; and all the time he was squawking:

"My ring! My ruby! My ring!"

Orfeo lifted the stable lantern from its hook and, holding it close, cast stone after stone from the crushed bed to the floor, till he came to the jackdaw's nest, squashed as flat as a pancake. In it something glowed as red as an ember.

Orfeo took it up and held it close to the lantern. It was a great ruby, set in a small golden ring. The ruby was cut like a half-open rose, and round it in letters of gold ran the name, *Roselle*.

"It is mine, O, Orfeo! It is mine!" squawked the jackdaw, taking flying, pecking leaps at it.

"Since when did jackdaws wear rings?" asked Orfeo. "And since when is your name Roselle?"

"Roselle is a princess," the jackdaw told him. "She put the ring down by her open window while she washed her hands. And the next thing I knew, I was flying home with it in my beak."

"The ring belongs to the princess, Jack, not to you," said Orfeo. "You must give it back at once."

"I could pop it on her window ledge when no one was looking," suggested the jackdaw hopefully.

"No," said Orfeo firmly, "for then someone innocent

might be blamed. You must give it back into her own hands."

"They will wring my neck," wailed the jackdaw. "O, Orfeo, you are my mother and my father. *You* give it back for me — they will not wring yours."

So Orfeo agreed to take the ring to the princess.

He set out at dawn, leaving his tumbledown cabin just as it was with the great hole in its wall. At noon he reached the gates of the king's town and wondered, as he made his way toward the king's palace, why he did not meet a soul.

But in the square in front of the palace he found men standing as close as ears of corn in a cornfield. Every upper window was crowded; and there was not a face in all that sea of faces that was not turned toward the palace.

Orfeo was so tall that, standing on his toes and craning his long neck, he could see right over all those tossing heads. What he saw was a long line of riders, all as gaudy as popinjays, passing in at the palace gates between two rows of footmen, all streamlined black and white, bowing away like penguins.

"Who are they?" Orfeo asked the man at the window overhead.

"Why, today's batch of princes returning the princess' ring," the other chuckled.

"Can she have lost so many?" Orfeo marvelled.

"One only," the other told him, chuckling still. "But the finder is to marry her and be king after the king; so everywhere rings are being found to left and right."

Flattening himself against the fronts of the houses, Orfeo edged his way toward the palace gates. When the last of the popinjay princes had ridden in, he, too, stepped forward.

At the sight of his tall, lean beanpole of a figure, clad in a peasant's smock and topped by a thatch of hair as rough as a rook's nest, a great bellow of good-natured laughter shook the crowd. The footmen lifted haughty noses and would have clashed the gates in his face; but when he opened his palm and showed them what was hidden there, their eyes started out of their heads, and they let him in.

In the grand presence chamber, Orfeo saw the king sitting hawk-eyed on his throne, while on a lower throne beside him sat a bright-haired princess, as small and charming as a golden-crested wren.

As each prince in turn came before the king, he bowed and told how he had found his ring, then knelt to place it on the finger of the princess. Each time, she sat and stared at the ring, then shook her bright head sadly; each time, a murmur passed round the chamber:

"The ring did not light up!"

At last only Orfeo was left. As he stepped forward to make his bow, titters swelled behind his back; and as, in his kind, slow brogue, he told his story, the popinjay princes rocked with laughter, while the king sat grim and tight-lipped, his eyes like a pair of gimlets.

But when Orfeo knelt and placed the ring on the Princess Roselle's finger, it flamed into such a sunburst of splendour that every face was washed by its crimson light; and this time the murmur grew to a roar:

"The right ring has been found!"

The princess lifted her bright head, and looked at Orfeo; and the smile she gave him went straight from her heart to his.

"Father," she said, "this is my ring; and this is the man I shall marry."

At this, the king's hair stood on end with temper, so

that his crown flew up, then fell back on his head with a plop.

"What, marry a peasant?" he exploded. "Have you taken leave of your senses? Away with you, miss, to the Rose Tower till you find them again! As for you, my fine beetle-tamer, you can thank your stars I am letting you off with merely kicking you out of my palace!"

Rough hands seized Orfeo and dragged him out of the royal presence. Hearty kicks sped him out of the palace gates. He went by back ways to the gates of the town, and sat down to think in the shelter of the buttress that held up its wall.

Soon people came running to the town gates, to see the princess pass on her way out to the Rose Tower.

"Mother, what *is* a Rose Tower?" Orfeo heard a child's shrill voice ask.

"It is where the king shuts people up till they do what he tells them," the mother answered.

"I should run away if he put *me* there," said the child.

"No one yet has ever got out of the Rose Tower," his mother told him. "It is right on the edge of a cliff, and it has three high walls all round it. Look — look! Here she comes!"

Murmurs of pity and love rose from the crowd as the princess' litter was carried past, with guards on either hand.

"But there are two princesses in it, Mother," piped the child, "both with golden hair."

"The one this side is the princess," his mother told him. "The other is Lady Rosina, her cousin and lady-in-waiting."

Behind this litter rumbled a wagon, laden with stores and clothing. Last of all walked two of the palace porters, carrying a big wicker basket between them by its ear-shaped handles.

"What is that basket for, Mother?" the child piped up again.

"For the roses," his mother told him. "Red roses bloom about the Rose Tower all the year round. When the princess fills that basket with roses and sends it to the king, it will tell him she has given in, and then he will let her out."

"I wish *I* had that basket. It would be lovely to hide in," said the child.

Hidden behind his buttress, Orfeo could have jumped for joy. The child's chatter had shown him just how to rescue the princess.

When the crowd had drifted home, Orfeo rose and followed the wagon's wheel tracks out of the town and through the forest to the cliff top. He saw how the tower and its rose garden were hemmed in by its three high walls. He could quite see why no one yet had ever got away.

"But no one till now," he said to himself, "has had the help of a beetle-tamer and his winter guests."

He tramped back to his tumbledown home and held a council of war with his guests. A clapping of wings, paws, front legs, greeted the plan he put before them.

"O, Orfeo, you are our mother and our father," they all chanted. "For you we would do far, far more than this."

So off Orfeo sent the jackdaw to tell Roselle and Rosina his plan. Landing on the window ledge at the top of the Rose Tower, the jackdaw thrust in his saucy head at the open casement and squawked:

"Princess, Orfeo is coming to rescue you with thousands and thousands of friends."

Roselle and Rosina ran to the window. Their faces grew bright with hope as they nodded their golden heads at each point in the plan the jackdaw unfolded.

When the jackdaw had flown away, Rosina helped the princess into her royal robes of purple velvet. She set her golden crown on her golden head, and her ruby ring on her finger. Then Rosina withdrew to the bedchamber.

The princess rang a silver bell. She was alone when two guards answered it.

"I am ready to send the king my father his basket of roses," she said. "Bring them up here for me to set in order."

She was still alone when they brought the basket, heaped high with red roses.

"Send the porters up in half an hour," she told them, "to take the basket to the palace."

As soon as the guards had gone, Rosina ran in from the bedchamber. Barring the door, they tipped out the roses and swiftly changed clothes. Wrapped in a rose-coloured cloak, the princess curled up in the bottom of the basket, and Rosina heaped the roses over her. Those that were left over she hid inside an old oak chest.

When, half an hour later, the porters knocked at the door, it was already unbarred, and Rosina was standing before the window, her back to the light, clad in Roselle's royal robes of purple velvet, Roselle's golden crown on her own golden head. The great ruby flashed on her finger as she motioned them to take the basket. If asked, they would have sworn it was the princess herself they had seen.

The porters took up the basket of roses, and carried it down spiral after spiral of the corkscrew stairs. The guards unlocked the brazen door of the tower and the gates of the three high walls for them; and out they passed into the forest, the basket of heaped roses swinging between them.

They walked in silence for a while. Then one of them said:

"It did not take the princess long to give in. A pity. I liked the look of that beetle-tamer."

"I, too," said the other. "He had the makings of our kind of king."

They walked in silence for a while further. Then the first said:

"Roses weigh heavier than you would think."

"There's a lot of iron in roses," said the second.

They walked in silence for a further while. Then the first, glancing up, gave a loud yelp of terror; and the second, glancing down, gave one even louder.

For from side to side, as far as the eye could reach, the air was thick with birds and beetles, in their thousands and their thousands of thousands, all flying toward them as fast as their wings could carry them.

And from side to side, as far as the eye could reach, the ground was covered with every kind of small, four-footed creature, in their thousands and their thousands of thousands, all racing toward them with teeth bared and the most bloodthirsty look on their innocent furry faces.

"Run for love of your life!" cried both porters together.

And they dropped the basket of roses and ran as if all the fiends in the world were at their heels, as indeed they thought they were.

Then out from among the trees rode Orfeo on a shaggy wild pony, leading its twin by a halter of heather rope. He scattered the blanket of red roses on the grass; he scooped up the princess in her rose-coloured cloak; he set her on her pony; and away they galloped to his tumbledown home.

Orfeo sent off the jackdaw at once to tell the king their news.

"Well, well! There is more in my beetle-tamer," cried the king, "than in all those popinjay princes!"

And he laughed at this turning of the tables on himself till his crown slipped rakishly askew. Then he sent back word by the jackdaw that Roselle and her beetle-tamer were to come home to his palace at once and have a fine wedding, with Rosina as chief bridesmaid.

This they did; and when, in due course, the king died, Orfeo became king after him. He was a king after every man's heart; and throughout the land and all his long life his people called him in love King Beetle-Tamer.

Ogo and the Sun Horse

Malvaizia was a wicked old witch. She was as wrinkled as a walnut, and as grey as the grey mist; her cold eyes were as lidless as a lizard's; for hair she had hanks of drab seaweed; and the gnashing of her teeth was like the whirr and grind of millstones.

She lived in a cave on the seashore with Ogo, her light-fingered rascal of a son. When she sat with one foot on the sand and the other in the sea, she could put spells on both land and water.

She wore a captive octopus draped like a cloak about her craggy shoulders, its head behind her own like a hood. Stuck in her belt of sea-serpent skin were the three sharpest things in the world — a bodkin made out of a crab's claw, a spindle made out of shark's teeth, and a swordfish's sword.

"Read me my fortune, Old Crone," Ogo said to his mother one day.

Malvaizia took her bodkin from her belt and prodded the octopus with it.

"Squirt!" she barked.

The octopus squirted. It squirted a jet of sepia into the rock basin at the mouth of the cave. Over this ink pool the old witch bent and stared, without a wink or a blink of her cold lizard eyes, into its murky depths.

"Ogo, my son!" she chortled. "Do you know that you will be the very first man to go right around the world in twenty-three hours?"

"Shall I, indeed?" snorted Ogo. "And how and when shall I die?"

Again the old witch bent and stared, without a wink or a blink of her cold lizard eyes, into the murky depths of the ink pool.

"You are due to die in a sword test," she reported. "But you can sidestep that if you kidnap a small wind."

"Pooh! Nothing easier," boasted Ogo.

And away he went, bounding and bouncing, till he came to Windy Corner.

This was where the winds who were the air's charwomen lived. Their babies swung, tucked up cosily in leafy cradles, from the boughs of all its bushes, rocking and sleeping peacefully while their mothers were out at work, sweeping the clouds from the sky and the fallen leaves from the fields.

Now Ogo lived by stealing; he even lived *for* stealing. For light fingers there was not his match in the whole world. So to him it was nothing, nothing at all, to snatch a small wind from its cradle. He kidnapped it so skilfully and smoothly that he had it out and away and home in his cave and it did not even wake.

Malvaizia took it from him, popped it into a bladder of bladder-wrack, and hung the tiny seaweed sack among her seaweed hair.

"Hide one among many," she cackled, "and who will see it there?"

"Aie! Aie!" mourned a mother-wind, sweeping by with streaming hair and streaming eyes. It was the mother-wind who had just gone home to Windy Corner and found her cradle empty. Her eyes passed unseeing over her small wind's prison; and on she went, moaning, to and fro, to and fro about the world, seeking her child, pouncing on each small sound in the frantic hope that this, this might be her lost darling.

"Who will see it there indeed?" smirked Ogo, and he winked and slapped his thigh.

Ogo was such a master thief that his cave was chock-a-block with stolen treasures of every size and shape and colour and sort and kind. As he was roaming and rootling among them later that day, he suddenly yawned and said:

"I have stolen every single thing worth stealing within a day's march of this hole. Look in your ink pool, Old Crone, and find me some more to loot."

"Find them yourself," snapped Malvaizia. "Why don't you steal a horse from the sun? It will carry you right around the Earth in twenty-three hours, and there won't be a thing worth stealing in the whole world that you won't see."

"I'll do that, so I will!" cried Ogo briskly, and he slapped his thigh again.

A quickbeam tree grew on the cliff above the cave. Up the cliff climbed Malvaizia, clinging with tooth and nail, and cut a switch from it with her sharp fish-sword.

"Nothing keeps an enchanted horse in order like a quickbeam switch," she told Ogo as she handed it over. "Here, you had better take my fish-sword, too. Nothing else will be sharp enough to cut that horse's traces."

Ogo took them both; and away he went, bounding and bouncing, toward the East, for he knew that it was only at Sunrise Point that the sun's chariot paused awhile. On he went, bounding and bouncing, bouncing and bounding, till he came to a rose bush bearing two golden roses and beside it a wheat stalk bearing two golden ears of wheat. A stream of clear water flowed nearby. And so he knew he had come to Sunrise Point.

He wriggled himself right under a rock, like a creeping thing. Night fell. All night long he lay here and, one by one, felt the three colds of night creep upon him. First it grew as cold as a coffin, and he knew from this that it was midnight. Then it grew as cold as a wind blowing under a sail, and he knew from this that it was three o'clock, when the Earth's breathing changes. Then it grew as cold as Malvaizia's eyes, and he knew from this that dawn was at hand.

And then Ogo saw the sun's golden chariot approaching. He heard the sun calling out to the two sun horses who pulled the chariot to pause and rest awhile. So the horses paused by the stream of clear water, and stooped their golden necks, and drank their fill. The sun stepped down from his golden chariot and groomed each horse in turn. He plucked the two golden roses and braided them into their manes; he plucked the two golden wheat ears and braided them into their tails. And at once the next dawn's two roses began to bud on the rose bush, and on the wheat stalk the next dawn's two wheat ears began to swell.

When the sun went around to the far side of his horses, Ogo wriggled out from beneath his stone and crept nearer, his body rippling along the ground like a snake's. One slash with Malvaizia's fish-sword, and he had cut the nearer steed free of his traces; one leap, and he bestrode him; one flick of the quickbeam switch, and *whish-whoosh* went the golden wings of the golden sun horse as he sprang and soared into flight.

No wind in the whole wide world could equal the speed of that sun horse. So swift and so strong was his flight, Ogo felt no more than a wisp of straw on his back. His knees gripping the horse's flanks as close as its bark grips a tree, away he went, away, away, around the stupendous race course of the sky.

And away around the course of the sky in his wake the sun drove, frantic and furious. But the sun's golden chariot was too heavy for only one horse; it tilted and tipped and rocked and rolled and staggered; farther and farther and ever farther it fell behind.

Everywhere on the Earth below, men cried out at the sight of the golden sun horse and his rider sweeping *whish-whoosh* overhead, at the sight of the sun in his chariot toiling painfully in the rear. And everywhere on the Earth below, Ogo saw such treasures crying out to be stolen that his fingers itched to filch them then and there.

But the most priceless treasure of them all was the one he had already stolen. He knew that he could never bear to let this golden sun horse out of his hands again.

"In any case," he mused, "I shall need him for when I go a-robbing and a-raiding around the world."

So, as he came up from the other side of the Earth to Sunrise Point an hour before sunrise was due (for he had galloped around the Earth in only twenty-three hours), he turned his horse's head toward Malvaizia's cave.

As he flew over the quickbeam tree on the cliff above the cave, he gave the sun horse a vicious cut with the quickbeam switch, bringing him down to Earth with such a jar that it spilt a petal from the golden rose braided into his mane and jolted the golden wheat ear from his tail. Sparks flew from his golden hoofs as he galloped over the rocks. Then the cave swallowed his brightness.

Sunface, the sun's young cupbearer, his face as bright as the golden goblet in his hands, had come in the night to Sunrise Point, bringing wine to comfort the sad heart of his lord. As he stood waiting, he felt, one by one, the first two colds of night creep upon him.

First it grew as cold as a coffin; and he knew from this that it was midnight. Then it grew as cold as a wind blowing under a sail; and he knew from this that it was three o'clock, when the Earth's breathing changes.

But before the third cold crept upon him, the sky grew red with a false and fleeting sunrise, as Ogo on his sun horse came galloping up from the other side of the Earth. He came in a flash; he went in a flash; he came and went too swiftly to note the bright face and the bright cup gleaming softly between the rose bush and the wheat staff. He came and went too swiftly for Sunface to stop him in mid-flight, but the eye of Sunface followed the flash and marked the way he went.

After a while it grew as cold as Malvaizia's eyes; and Sunface knew from this that the time for the true dawn was at hand. Yet still the true dawn tarried a while longer, till at last the sun came toiling up the sky with one weary sun horse. It had taken him twenty-five hours to drive around the Earth.

When the sun had gratefully drained the golden wine cup, Sunface begged a boon:

"Lord, give me leave to follow the horse thief and bring your sun horse home."

"Stretch forth your right palm," replied the sun. "I will give you a gift for the road."

Sunface stretched forth his right palm. The sun touched it with the light that streamed from his own finger tips.

"On the Earth it is hard to tell truth from lies," he said. "But if any Earth-being lies to you now, your right palm will spurt fire."

The sun horse harnessed to the chariot drank his fill from the clear stream, but without joy, for his heart was heavy with the loss of his friend. Sunface groomed him; he plucked one of the golden roses and braided it into his mane; he plucked one of the golden wheat ears and braided it into his tail. And at once a second rose began to bud beside the rose left on the rose bush, and beside the wheat ear left on the wheat stalk a second wheat ear began to swell.

Then the sun took up his golden reins and drove his chariot on to bring day to the western world; and Sunface, as light and as bright and as fleet and as neat as a sunbeam, went speeding in the direction in which he had seen Ogo and the stolen sun horse flashing by.

A lingering line of faint and fading brightness in the air led him as far as the quickbeam tree on the cliff above the cave; but here the brightness ended as abruptly as if cut off with a knife. As he stood beneath the tree, looking searchingly about him, he saw that one of its branches had been severed, and he drew his sword that the touch of its sunbeam blade might heal the wound. At the rattle of the scabbard the mother-wind, in sudden hope, came sweeping up from the seashore.

"Aie! Aie!" she moaned when her eyes fell on Sunface. "It is you, Sunface, not my little lost child. If you are seeking the stolen sun horse, I heard the *whish-whoosh* of his wings just here in the night, and the clang of his hoofs on the rocks by the witch's cave. It is strange how my heart keeps drawing me back to that cave. Come with me; I will show you."

Sunface followed her down the cliff, his bright face flashing a streak of light on the air, so that Ogo, peering from the cave, exclaimed:

"Look, Old Crone! A star is falling to the Earth!"

"Better if it were," cried Malvaizia as she joined him. "That is the face of the sun's cupbearer, hot on the tracks of his horse. Quick, let me get out and put one foot on sand and one in the sea, to spin a spell to save your new treasure!"

So, when Sunface had followed the mother-wind down to the seashore, what should he find there but a grey old woman sitting on a rock, with one bare foot on the sand and the other in the sea, her seaweed hair covering her from top to toe, and a captive octopus draped like a cloak about her craggy shoulders, its head behind her own like a hood. There she sat, spinning a seaweed cord on her sharp sharks-tooth spindle, muttering away to herself, grinning and grimacing and gnashing her huge teeth with a whirr and grind of millstones.

"Good be about you!" Sunface saluted her gravely.

She gave no greeting back, but went on with her baleful muttering. All she gave him was a look, and that look was as ugly as a bad deed.

But the mother-wind's grief-sharpened ears caught a fainter sound from the base of Malvaizia's rock. Down to it she blew in sudden hope, blew aside the concealing strands of seaweed hair, blew up into the hand of Sunface the golden rose petal the witch had been scraping into the sand with her bare heel.

"Aie! Aie!" mourned the mother-wind, for it was not her lost darling, after all.

Not a wink, not a blink, did those lizard eyes give; nor did the witch for an instant cease muttering and spluttering, grinning and grinding, spinning and spell binding.

But again the mother-wind's grief-sharpened ears had caught a delicate sound — a slight dry rustle amid the damp slap and flap of the seaweed turning the twisting, coiling and cording, on the sharks-tooth spindle. Up to it she blew with hope again renewed, taking the seaweed cord in her teeth, shaking it till it snapped; and out of it fell, right at the feet of Sunface, a golden ear of wheat.

"Aie! Aie!" mourned the mother-wind, for again it was not her lost darling.

Still not a wink, not a blink, did those lizard eyes give. But the muttering and the spluttering ceased, and the grinning and the grinding ceased; for the seaweed cord had snapped, and with it the spell the old witch had been spinning.

At last Sunface spoke again:

"Lady, where is your son?"

They say that an ostrich can hatch her egg with a look. That was the sort of look the old witch gave Sunface then, so piercing that it could have cracked an egg.

"My house is near, but my son is far," she snapped.

At once Sunface felt his right palm spurt fire.

"Not so far as he has been, I think," he said. "Has he not lately been all around the world?"

And he began to walk toward the cave.

At this the old witch gave a warning cackle, which brought Ogo running at top speed out of the cave.

"What do you want of me?" he shouted angrily.

"A stolen sun horse," Sunface told him mildly.

"Horse?" blustered Ogo. "There are no horses here."

A second time Sunface felt his right palm spurt fire.

"Surely I hear one stamping," he said, as a clatter came from the cave.

"That is my grindstone," Ogo barked back.

A third time Sunface felt his right palm spurt fire.

"Surely I hear one whinnying," he said; and this time it was so plain that even Ogo could not deny it.

"That is a seahorse out in the bay," he blustered again.

A fourth time Sunface felt his right palm spurt fire.

"Let us put this to the sword test," he challenged. "We will both fling up our swords. The sword of the one who speaks truth will fall *before* him; the sword of the one who lies will fall *on* him."

Malvaizia nodded vigorously, looking as smug as a cat who has licked the cream-pot clean. All that had been obscure in the ink pool was now clear to her. Under her seaweed hair her right hand sought her bodkin, and her left hand sought the bladder in which the small wind was hidden.

Sunface flung up his sun sword. It left an arc in the air that shimmered like a rainbow. Point downward it fell and stood upright and quivering in the sand before his feet.

Ogo flung up his fish-sword. Malvaizia pricked the bladder, and, with a whimper, out rushed the little wind. *Puff* went the little wind; it was just the right size, as well Malvaizia knew, to blow Ogo's sword a pace forward into safety as it fell.

But the mother-wind had heard her lost darling's cry. She blew headlong to embrace it; and the rush of her coming blew the sword briskly back. It fell, point downward, on Ogo; Ogo fell lifeless on the sand.

At this, Malvaizia rose, shrieking, and the octopus hanging from her craggy shoulders began to stir its arms. A mighty wave swept in and over the rock; when it was sucked noisily back, Ogo and Malvaizia were there no longer, and something which looked like a giant starfish was floating out to sea.

While the mother-wind blew blithely home to Windy Corner, her darling in her arms, Sunface went into the cave. Out he led the golden sun horse; onto his back he leaped. *Whish-whoosh* went the golden wings; a streak of light flashed upward through the air; Sunface had no need of a quickbeam switch to urge on his eager steed.

At Sunrise Point, when at dawn the sun came up from the other side of the Earth, there was an interchange of joyful whinnyings. Blissfully the two sun horses drank together from the stream; blissfully Sunface groomed them, braiding a fresh rose into each mane, into each tail a fresh wheat ear; blissfully he watched the sun set out on his radiant journey. Everywhere, grateful and rejoicing, trees lifted up their arms, and men their faces, and blessed the sun and his cupbearer who had restored their world to order. And once more the golden chariot drove around the Earth in twenty-four hours, and has done so ever since.

Roll Away the Stone

Marigold was a small child, bare from top to toe, when she fell into the forest. She fell with a bump; all in an instant, where she was, there she was.

It was dark; all around her was only gloom as grey as ashes, between trees as black as soot. And it was lonely; there was nobody with her in the forest but herself.

Then, far off among the trees, she saw a spark of light. Far off or near, she ran toward it as fast as her little bare legs could carry her.

The spark grew into a little house, all a-glinting and a-glowing. Peeping in at the low window, Marigold saw a fire leaping merrily on the hearth, as if it were very glad to be alive. Before it a white doe lay stretched contentedly. There were red candles burning brightly on a table, with supper laid around them on a linen cloth so white that it shone.

In the firelight and the candlelight a lady sat at her purring spinning wheel. Her face was so motherly that all at once Marigold felt comforted.

As Marigold stood and stared in at the peaceful room, eating it up with her eyes, the white doe lifted her head, ears pricked, toward the window; and at this the lady rose from her spinning and came to the door and opened it.

"Who is there?" she called softly into the night.

"Marigold," gulped Marigold.

"Come in by the warm fire, Marigold," said the lady kindly.

She bent and drew her in, all bare from top to toe; she sat her by the fire beside the white doe; she tucked her up in a snug, soft shawl; she brought her hot milk to drink.

Kneeling beside her, smiling, she touched the beauty spot, that was like a tiny marigold, between Marigold's eyebrows.

"Now I know why you are called Marigold," she said. "*My* name is Bona. Where do you come from, Marigold?"

Marigold thought hard.

"I can *nearly* remember, but not quite." she said at last.

"*How* did you come, Marigold?" Bona asked her then.

"A big bird dropped me," Marigold told her promptly.

There was a torn strip of fine linen clutched in Marigold's left hand. Bona drew it gently out and held it to the fire to examine it. It was exquisitely woven, in a design she had never seen before, with a gold thread fringing the flax.

Staring through it at the fire, Bona saw a picture forming in the flames. She saw Marigold running up a flight of marble steps from a sunny lake in which she had been bathing; she saw her waving the towel in her hand at someone nearby; she saw a griffin swoop, attracted by the glitter of the golden fringe; she saw the tussle, and the towel tearing, and Marigold snatched up in the griffin's claws and carried high over the plains and forests — who could tell how many leagues?

Marigold was lost; it would be impossible to find the way back to her home. But Bona lifted the lid of the big cedarwood chest in which she kept her woven stuffs, and she laid the linen fragment carefully away with them.

Marigold stayed with Bona and became her foster child. Bona spun and wove garments for her, strong and gaily coloured, fitted to the carefree life she led, playing with the white doe, running happily in and out of the little forest house, helping Bona to keep it all a-glinting and a-glowing, gathering herbs in her garden and apples in her orchard.

"Do not stray too far into the forest, Marigold," Bona warned her one day, "in case you meet a tiger."

"Would a tiger not be friends with me?" asked Marigold in surprise. "The deer and the hares and the birds and the squirrels all are."

"We have wild beasts in the forests, too," Bona told her. "It is one of the king's hunting forests. Just in case you do ever meet one, we will cut you a hazel wand at the next full moon."

The orchard had a hedge of hazel bushes all round it, and at the full of the moon Bona and Marigold went along this with a silver knife. The bushes wagged to and fro in the moonlight; and Bona looked each bush over till she found the most pliant bough of all — so pliant a bough that, when she cut it, it twisted around itself till it looked like a rod with two snakes twined about it.

"Carry it always in your girdle," Bona said as she gave it to Marigold, "and if any wild beast bares his teeth at you, hold it firmly in your right hand and touch his heart with it."

"And what will *he* do then?" asked Marigold a little breathlessly.

"Oh, then," said Bona, "he will be your friend."

That night, as Bona and Marigold slept, an earth-quake shook the forest. The little forest house fell in, so that its roof timbers lay lower than its floor timbers, its floor higher than its roof. When dawn came and Marigold crawled out from amid the wreckage, Bona and her white doe were nowhere to be seen.

Near and far Marigold sought for them, calling their names with a breaking heart. As she wandered to and fro in her search, she found that the very face of the forest had changed. Fallen trees lay like barriers across the green paths along which she used to run; the clear springs at which she used to drink had been swallowed up. And at one place where there had been a landslide she came upon a cave that had been opened up and laid bare.

"The little forest house is gone," thought Marigold. "I will make this cave my new home. At least it will give me shelter."

So to this cave she took whatever she could salvage from the ruins of the little house that had been all a-glinting and a-glowing. The big cedarwood chest she had to leave, for it lay smashed; but she was glad to empty it of Bona's woven stuffs to add a little warmth and cheer to her new bare home of rock. A rotting fragment of gold-fringed linen which was caught on the splintered wood was all she left behind.

As she knelt presently in that new bare home of rock, coaxing a spark from flint and steel to light a fire, it suddenly went darker. Whirling round, she saw that the lower part of the mouth of the cave was blocked and two green points were burning in the gloom.

"Who is there?" she called out bravely, though her voice *did* tremble a little.

The bulk blocking the entrance moved farther into the cave; and as the light streamed in again Marigold saw a huge wild beast regarding her with green eyes blazing and sharp teeth bared. His orange coat was striped with black.

"*Tiger* is here," he growled, deep in his throat. "And who are you?"

And he made his whiskers fierce and bristled his tawny beard at her.

"Marigold," gulped Marigold, shaking with fright.

But even in her fear she remembered Bona's warning, and her right hand flew to the hazel wand in her girdle.

"Are you not afraid that I shall eat you, Marigold?" the tiger growled again, lashing his tail and unsheathing his cruel claws while his body crouched, ready to spring.

"Not w-while I have my hazel w-wand," stammered Marigold, holding it firmly and pointing it straight at his heart.

At this all the wickedness ran out of the tiger, just like sawdust stuffing. He yawned a homely fireside yawn, stretched himself lazily and lay down, as relaxed and happy as a pet cat on a warm hearth-rug.

Marigold leaned forward and touched with her hazel wand the place where she thought a tiger would keep his heart. His whiskers twitched and twinkled with pleasure, and he smiled most amiably.

"This is a fine cave," he purred. "Two could live here and be good company. Let us set up house in it together, and I will be your Uncle Tiger and take care of you."

They set up house together in the cave, and Uncle Tiger became as fussy about Marigold's safety as an old hen with one chick. He prowled about the forest till he found a boulder just the right size for a fine front door, and this between them they pushed and pulled till they got it home in triumph to the mouth of the cave.

"Each time I have to go out on tiger-business, Marigold," he told her, "you must shut yourself indoors, and you must not open our fine front door till you hear me calling, *Marigold, Marigold, roll away the stone!* Now promise me, across your heart."

And across her heart she promised him.

Next day, while Uncle Tiger was out on tiger-business, Marigold heard such an uproar in the forest as she had never heard before in all her born days. She crouched cowering over the cave fire and blessed their fine front door, for it sounded as if all the wild beasts in the world were rampaging on the other side of it.

It was like music in her ears when at last she heard Uncle Tiger growl:

"Marigold, Marigold, roll away the stone!"

She ran to obey; and in staggered Uncle Tiger, puffing and panting and weary to the bone.

The very second he was inside, he closed their fine front door, then threw himself down before the fire, and purred with pride like a kettle on the boil:

"I led the king a fine dance today, when he came hunting in *my* forest! Did you hear his hounds yelping, and his horses thudding, and his huntsmen shouting, and his horns going, *Tantivy, Tantivy*? If they were swift, your Uncle Tiger was swifter!"

"Oh, Uncle Tiger, *don't* go out tomorrow!" Marigold begged, alarmed. "You have saved yourself the first time, but you mightn't do so the second. What would I do if the king were to kill you?"

"Tush, my dear; first he would have to catch me," said Uncle Tiger. "But do not hang your bright little head and dim your beauty spot with worry. There will not be a second time, for the king never stays here more than one day. He will be hunting in some other tiger's forest tomorrow."

40

And so indeed the king had planned to do.

But as he and his huntsmen sat round their campfire that evening, eating before riding away, they fell to telling stories of the day's sport; and if the first story was far-fetched, those which followed were even more so, so that the shouts of laughter grew louder with each one.

Presently one of the huntsmen said:

"Now this is as true as that I sit here in this forest. I was hard on the tiger's heels when he reached his den. A rock blocked its entrance. That tiger called on a flower to roll away the stone; and this rock moved, and the tiger went in, and the rock moved back."

Again his comrades shouted with laughter, then challenged one who had not yet spoken:

"Outfly *that* flight of fancy if you can!"

"Believe this or not," he replied, "but in this tumbledown forest I found a tumbledown orchard; and in this tumbledown orchard I found a tumbledown house; and in this tumbledown house I found a tumbledown chest; and in this tumbledown chest I found — *this!*"

And out of his hunting pouch he pulled a strip of rotting linen with a fringe of tarnished gold.

"Well-tried!" cried his comrades, shouting with laughter again.

But one of them stretched out his hand for the strip of linen. He held it to the firelight to examine it, as Bona had done when Marigold first came to her. He rose and came to the king; and a sudden silence fell on the rest of the men.

"Sire," he said, "my wife is the queen's towel-weaver. I know this pattern well. This is the fringe of a towel woven for the royal nursery. It was a fringe exactly like this that had been torn off the towel the Princess

Marigold's nurse brought back from the lake the day the griffin carried Princess Marigold away."

"Marigold?" repeated the huntsman who had told the story of the tiger's den. "That is the flower the tiger called on — *Marigold, Marigold, roll away the stone!*"

Everyone held his breath, awaiting the king's reply.

"We sleep here tonight," said the king.

If the sun was up early next morning, the king was earlier.

"Dig a trap for that tiger out of earshot of his den," he ordered his huntsmen. "Snare him alive and unharmed, and take him back to his den."

Then to the huntsman who had found the cave he said:

"Now lead me to this den."

The huntsman did so, then led the king's horse away, while the king hid himself in a nearby tree from which he could keep watch on the mouth of the cave. For a while nothing happened; no one went in; no one came out. Then, as day followed dawn, the rock at the cave mouth moved. Out came the tiger and stood waiting and watching while the rock moved back again.

Uncle Tiger sniffed the air, and smelled the good smell of the goat the huntsmen had tethered in their trap as bait. Away he paced toward it, advancing through his forest like a lord.

When he had passed out of earshot, the king came down from the tree, and went and stood before the cave. Making his voice like a tiger's — at least, as far as he was able — he called out:

"Marigold, Marigold, roll away the stone!"

The stone was rolled away. The king went in.

A young girl stood before him, so like his queen in her own girlhood that his heart turned over. But there was one difference — between her eyebrows shone the beauty spot like a tiny marigold which had given his long-lost daughter her name.

Marigold, trembling a little at the sight of a human form instead of Uncle Tiger's, snatched her hazel wand from her girdle and pointed it toward him. Then, as she met his eyes, memory and joy flashed up in her own, and she flew into his arms like a bird.

The king's horse was led to the mouth of the cave; the king was just lifting Marigold into the saddle when the huntsmen hauled back Uncle Tiger, snarling but unharmed, on a strong leash. As soon as he saw Marigold on horseback, Uncle Tiger snapped his leash as if it were of cobweb and bounded up to her, his whiskers all on end.

"Where my niece goes, I go," he growled. "Or whom will she have to take care of her?"

So, seated before her father on his horse, with her father's arm about her, her hazel wand safe in her girdle, and her Uncle Tiger pacing majestically beside her, Marigold went home.

The Root of Healing

The hare was the forest doctor. His name was Dr Bobtail, but all the animals called him Dr Bob. He used to be able to cure every forest sickness under the sun; then all at once his forest cures stopped working, just like that.

Two of his largest patients, the lion and the she-bear, came to put their heads together with his about it.

"The whole forest is taking to its bed," said Leonardo-Leonides. (That was the lion.) "Look at Ursula here; you never saw such a bear-with-a-sore-head as she has been for months."

"And look at Leonardo's mane," put in Ursula Bruin. (That was the she-bear.) "It keeps coming out in pawfuls. He will soon be as bald as a bone."

"If anyone can save the forest," said Dr Bob, twitching his whiskers in his gravest bedside manner, "it will be Mafanda. Let us go and see if she will."

Mafanda was the head forester's young daughter, and a bosom friend of all the forest beasts. She and her puppy Thomasina listened with round eyes (and Thomasina with one ear cocked as well) while Dr Bob told them how his forest cures had suddenly stopped working just like that.

"What made them stop?" asked Mafanda.

"All this death-dust in the air has killed my Root of Healing," Dr Bob explained. "And without a pinch of that in it, how *can* a forest cure work?"

"Couldn't you get another?" Mafanda suggested.

"Only from the Castle of the Night," Dr Bob told her. "And only with help from the stars."

"I have a cousin forty-two times removed who lives in the Zodiac," remarked Leonardo-Leonides. "I feel sure Cousin Leo would help us, if only I could get up to him."

"And I have a great-uncle living near the Pole Star," added Ursula Bruin. "I am only a poor relation, but I feel sure Uncle Ursa Major would help us, too, if only I could get up to him."

"My mother told me," confided the puppy Thomasina, thumping her tail on the grass, "that Sirius the Dog Star is my great-great-grandpapa. I would ask *him* to help us, if only I could get up to him."

"But how would you keep *this* Root of Healing alive if you got it, Dr Bob?" Mafanda asked.

"The Hare in the Moon is a distant connection of mine," replied Dr Bob, "and he knows the secret of immortality. I feel sure he would advise me, if only I could get up to him."

"I could take you all in my sleep ship," offered Mafanda.

"Oh, Mafanda, it is far too small," yelped Thomasina. "Why, that round bone box you keep it in is no bigger than your head!"

"Didn't your mother tell you, Thomasina," Mafanda teased her, "what happens to a sleep ship as soon as it is dark?"

As soon as it was dark, Mafanda took out her tiny sleep ship from its round bone box; and at once it began to grow. It grew and it grew; it grew all ways at once till there was room for them all in it, and elbow and tail room, too.

They all lay down on its deck. A gentle wind puffed

out its sail, and away they sailed, slowly, smoothly, across the Sea of Quiet Breathing, under the lee of the Hills of Slumber, and so into the vast Ocean of the Sky.

In this ocean's calm blue waters, the stars lay scattered like small golden islands. Among them, a larger silver island, floated the full moon.

On its shore stood the Hare in the Moon, stirring a bubbling brew of heavenly herbs with a silver spoon as tall as himself.

"Cousin Moon," called Dr Bob, "how can the Root of Healing stay alive on the death-dusty Earth?"

"Plant it in moss from a millpond, Cousin Bobtail," replied the Hare in the Moon, stirring away for dear life. "Keep it fresh with south-running water, scooped up against the flow of the stream. Feed it with the yellow star jelly that falls from the clouds. Let the sun shine on it; let the four winds blow on it; and it will stay alive."

The sleep ship sailed on between the golden islands to the one which was the home of Ursa Major, the Great Bear. He was just setting out with his wagon and horses for a leisurely drive around the Pole Star.

"Great-uncle Ursa," called Ursula Bruin, "how do you get into the Castle of the Night?"

"Knock three times on its outer gate with a star whip, Grand-niece Ursula," the Great Bear replied. "You had better have mine."

And he handed her his star whip.

The sleep ship threaded its way between the golden islands to the great Zoo Circle, the Zodiac. Here the mighty Leo was lying, crunching the crusty, fresh-baked loaves that lay heaped between his paws.

"Cousin Leo," called Leonardo-Leonides, "where in the Castle of the Night do you find the Root of Healing?"

"By the well in the inner garden, Cousin Leonardo-

Leonides," Leo told him. "Two cousins of ours guard the garden door; but they will let you pass if you give them each a star loaf. You had better take two of mine."

And he handed him two star loaves.

The sleep ship still sailed on till it came to an island shaped like a boat. Sirius the Dog Star stood like a captain at its prow, keeping his blue-white star watch.

"Great-great-grandpapa," called Thomasina, "if you get into the Castle of the Night, how do you get out?"

"Be out by the last stroke of midnight, dear great-great-grandchild," Sirius told her. "You had better have my star watch."

And he handed her his star watch.

On they sailed; and at last they reached the Castle of the Night. Its walls came right to the water's edge; little blue waves lapped dreamily against its outer gate.

Ursula Bruin stood up in the sleep ship and knocked three times with Ursa Major's whip. The gate swung open. Out of the sleep ship they stepped; in they all went.

On the far side of the wide courtyard two lions guarded a door. Leonardo-Leonides gave them each a loaf, and both lay quietly down to crunch them. The door behind them swung open. In they all went.

They came into a garden growing about a well. It was full of green and fragrant Roots of Healing. Thomasina began to dig up the nearest one with frantic nose and paws, while at her other end her tail wagged itself furiously. Mafanda stood over her with the star watch in her hand, her eyes fixed on the shining minute finger that was slowly creeping upright.

"*One!*" struck the star watch.

"Run!" shrieked Mafanda.

While the star watch went on striking, Dr Bob

scooped up the root, and back he loped like lightning. Back sprang Leonardo-Leonides. Back raced Mafanda. Back scuttled Thomasina. Back, last of all, waddled Ursula Bruin. "*Twelve!*" struck the star watch, and the outer gate shut on her tail hairs with a clap and a clash and a clang.

The wind of that clap-clash-and-clang blew them all aboard the sleep ship; it blew the sleep ship clean across the Ocean of the Sky and past the Hills of Slumber, over the Sea of Quiet Breathing and back to the shore of Earth.

Before they could say "Jack Robinson!" (supposing they had wanted to), it was tomorrow morning, the sleep ship had shrunk and folded its sails, and Mafanda had laid it away in its round bone box, no bigger than her head.

Together they planted the new Root of Healing in moss from a millpond. They kept it fresh with south-running water, scooped up against the flow of the stream. They fed it with the yellow star jelly that falls from the clouds. They let the sun shine on it; they let the four winds blow on it; they kept it alive.

Dr Bob put a pinch of it in all his forest cures; and at once they cured every forest sickness under the sun again, just like that.

The Prince Who Lost His Shadow

The king of a kingdom died suddenly, leaving an only son, Prince Pio, to succeed him. But before Prince Pio could do this, he lost his one and only shadow.

Now the way he lost his shadow was this:

Prince Pio had a stepmother; and although Prince Pio did not know it, this stepmother was a witch. This witch had a black cat named Maulkin; and although Prince Pio did not know it, this black cat was his stepmother's companion.

The day after the old king was buried, the queen-mother whipped Maulkin and sent her streaking widdershins around the church. *Widdershins* means the way the sun would go if it went backward; witches are fond of this way, for it brings natural laws into disorder and helps them to work bad magic.

"Quick, Pio!" the queen-mother shouted as if she were panic-stricken. "Catch Maulkin! It is forbidden for a cat to go running around a church."

So Prince Pio, who was well brought up and therefore obedient, ran around the church after Maulkin, and he was in such a hurry that he never noticed that he was running widdershins, which is a very dangerous way to run, for then your shadow falls behind you.

Now if a witch can step on your shadow while you are running widdershins around a church, she can tug it right away from you. And this is exactly what the queen-mother did with Prince Pio's, so that when he came back to her with Maulkin spitting and scratching and cursing and swearing in his arms, he was without his one and only shadow.

"Alas and alack, my son!" cried the queen-mother, making her eyes big and round as if with alarm. "What *have* you been doing? You have lost your one and only shadow!"

Prince Pio felt himself all over and looked all around himself for his shadow; but of course he could not find it, for the witch had folded it up as small and neat as a postage stamp and was holding it hidden in her palm.

"I feel just the same," he said. "Does it matter?"

"Matter?" she cried. "Of course it matters. By our old Celtic law a king must be perfect in every part, so you can never become king if you have no shadow. Off with you and search for it. *I* will look after the kingdom while you are away."

"If I am going hunting, I had better be dressed for hunting," thought Prince Pio.

So he put on thick brown leather hunting boots and a thick old green leather hunting jacket, and off he set to find his one and only shadow.

Now, where do you think that one and only shadow was? It was clenched between Maulkin's teeth as she flew through the air on her way to an Arabian sorcerer who lived in a castle on an island far across the sea. For Prince Pio's stepmother and this sorcerer were hand in glove together in a wicked plot to get Prince Pio's kingdom for themselves, and getting hold of his shadow was the first step in the plot.

Prince Pio went on walking till he reached the sea,

which stopped him walking any farther. The sun was just going down.

The seashore was deserted except for one old fisherman, who was painting a big, bold blue eye on the front of his little white boat. His green jersey, patched all over, had a hole under the right arm.

"Lashings of lions be in your path!" he greeted Prince Pio.

In Prince Pio's kingdom that was the polite way to greet a huntsman.

"And shoals of fishes in yours," Prince Pio greeted him back.

In Prince Pio's kingdom that was the polite way to return a fisherman's greeting.

"This would be a fine jersey," said the fisherman, treating himself to a straight back, "if only it had a patch under this arm. I suppose you haven't a spare patch about you?"

"Only patch pockets," said the prince. "Take one, and welcome."

The old fisherman pulled off one of Prince Pio's patch pockets and clapped it over the hole under his arm. It melted into the jersey as if it belonged.

"Ah!" said the old fisherman gleefully. "Now I can give my boat's weather eye such a bright blue iris that she will be able to find her own way wherever she has to go."

"Could she find her way to my shadow?" asked Prince Pio. "Did you notice I had lost it?"

"I did. She could. She shall," said the old fisherman.

He licked his brush to a fine point and dipped it in black paint; he painted the last curled eyelash and stepped back to admire it; he washed his brush in a rock pool and dried it on the princely patch under his arm.

"Jump in, curl up and go to sleep," he said. "With her weather eye open, my boat can travel both by daylight and by starlight as sure and straight as a bird."

"And when she gets there, wherever *there* is?" Prince Pio asked.

"Pull her up on dry land and turn her weather eye seaward," the old fisherman told him. "There she will wait like a faithful old dog to bring you and your shadow home. Aye, and more than your shadow, if what my new patch whispers turns out true."

Prince Pio, being well brought up and therefore obedient, jumped in, curled up and went to sleep. He did not wake as the boat rocked over the waves behind its bright blue weather eye. He did not wake when dusk fell. He did not wake when dusk deepened into dark. He did not wake till the prow jarred on a shingle beach. Then, he opened his eyes to see, high above him, a lighted castle jutting on a black and silver sky and blotting out the stars.

"Well," thought Prince Pio, "here I am, I know not where, nor how I am to find my shadow in wherever it is I am. Still, kill or cure, end or mend, up to this castle I must wend."

He drew up his boat on dry land and turned her weather eye seaward. Up, up, up through the night he climbed over shingle and rocks to the tall castle; and scarcely had he reached its torch-lit courtyard when two red lights like balls of fire rushed down out of the sky toward him.

As he flinched away into the shadows, they turned into cat's eyes. Then who should land neatly on her four black feet in that torch-lit courtyard but Maulkin! And who should step lightly down from Maulkin's back but

Prince Pio's stepmother, very queenly in her scarlet mantle and her golden crown!

Now Prince Pio was a dear, good, simple soul who never thought harm of anyone. So, though such a method of air travel made him scratch his head, he was just about to hail his stepmother warmly when the door of the castle swung open, and the Arabian sorcerer, tall and gaunt in his long black gown, his bald skull enclosed in a round black cap studded with gems, came stalking out to greet her. And his stepmother's first words made Prince Pio think twice about hailing her.

"You have fastened my stepson's shadow to his puppet?" she asked.

"I have," the sorcerer nodded.

"And they are both in the keeping of a pure and noble captive maiden?" she asked again.

Again the sorcerer nodded.

"All I need is your help," he said, "to bring the puppet to life. Then we can send it out at once to do such ill deeds in his name that the kingdom will gladly offer itself to us."

The queen mother lifted her head and sniffed the air.

"By pricking of my thumbs," she said, "he is already on his way here. So first let us go in and blast him to death with a whirlwind."

They went into the castle, Maulkin slinking between them, and the door closed with a clang behind them. But almost at once it burst open and, with a shrieking like that of lost souls, a whirlwind tore across the courtyard, blowing the torches into writhing ribbons of fire, and plunged down into the sea.

In the dark, Prince Pio could hear the roar of the churning waves as they piled into mountains, then dashed themselves to foam on the rocks below. Had he indeed been out on that lashing, crashing sea, he would certainly never have lived to tell the tale.

Then suddenly, above the tumult, he heard a sweet voice singing; and the fury of storm and whirlwind died gently away. As if by magic the full moon stood clear and bright in heaven; as if by magic, the sea slept peacefully beneath its light; seals lay on the rocks, enraptured by the singing; and fishes lifted their heads from the still water, mouths open with delight.

Prince Pio slipped around the castle till, craning his head backward, he saw, far above, the lighted window from which the singing came; leaning from it, framed in its light, were the head and shoulders of a girl.

Hand over hand and foot above foot, he climbed the stout ivy on the castle wall till he reached the open casement.

"Oh!" she cried then. "You are safe; you are safe, Prince Pio! The whirlwind did not blast you!"

And she drew him into the room.

"I am Phao," she told him. "The sorcerer holds me captive, for the presence of a maiden gives power to his spells. But, as you just saw, where I can I work to undo his evil enchantments."

"But why have you never climbed down the ivy and escaped?" he cried.

"There was no boat," she said. "Witches and sorcerers have swifter ways of travelling."

"There is a boat now," he whispered, taking her hand. Then, suddenly remembering, he exclaimed:

"You called me by my name! How did you know?"

"Come and see," she said.

Taking up the silver lamp which lit the room, Phao

led Prince Pio to a shadowy corner. He started at what the light revealed. For there, asleep on a silken divan, surely lay himself!

And yet, as he stared, he shuddered.

"Am I really like that?" he gasped.

"It is a most lying likeness," Phao comforted him. "For all that is good in you has here been turned to evil. And yet both form and features are your own. That is how I knew you were Prince Pio, for I heard the sorcerer chant your name when he fastened your shadow to your puppet."

"It was for my shadow I came," he told her. "If I do not get it back before my stepmother and the sorcerer bring this puppet to life, much evil will be loosed upon the world."

"I will help you," said Phao.

She held the lamp so that the prince's lost shadow slid aside from the puppet till it was fastened only at the feet.

"Pull. Pull hard," she cried.

Prince Pio grasped his shadow and pulled hard. It stood firm; it resisted. Then all at once it quivered; it tore free; it leaped to him and was his own again. And as this happened, the shape and the features of the puppet melted like mist, and on the divan lay only a formless block of wood.

Voices reached them from the spiral stairs that led up to Phao's turret — a man's and a woman's, the sorcerer's and the queen's.

"They are coming to bring the puppet to life," Phao whispered. "Quick, or we shall be too late."

She blew out the lamp, and out of the casement they went head first, and like lightning down the ivy. They were running hand in hand from the courtyard toward the beach when a tornado burst out of the castle and tossed them into the air like straws.

"They are raising a new whirlwind against us," gasped Phao. "I must send it back to them."

And again, most sweetly, she began to sing.

The whirlwind cast them down and threshed its way back to the castle. As they picked each other up and ran, they heard it batter down the doors. From the inner halls they heard clap after clap of thunder.

Together they pushed the boat down the beach to the lip of the tide and jumped in. Winking its weather eye, off it skimmed like a gull across the quiet water.

Looking back at the tall castle looming in the moonlight, they saw the courtyard torches toss and dive in the blasts of the whirlwind. They saw the rent walls gape; they saw flames that shot sky-high. Then the castle tottered and crashed among the flames with a jolt that shook the island.

But King Pio, under a sky growing pale with the coming dawn, was swiftly and joyfully taking his queen and his shadow home.

Unicorn's Fosterling

There was once, I am not sure when, in a far land, I am not sure where, a wizard skilled in every sort of sorcery. The more he got, the more he wanted, and the more he wanted, the more he got, till at last he said:

"There isn't a thing in life left to want, except not to die!"

He went into the desert, and drew symbols in the sand. The symbols shifted and shaped themselves into a secret script.

"That man need never die," he read, "who bears within himself the sun and the ruby of Amfortas."

Now the wizard knew where to find the sun any day of the week; but he did not know where to find the ruby of Amfortas. So he put himself to sleep, and sent himself out to find it.

Away down the years he went back — how far, who can say? — till he found the wounded King Amfortas in a castle on Mount Salvat. On his head was a cap of sables, worked with bands of Arabian gold. On the top of the cap flashed the ruby.

The wizard saw how the cap had decayed as the years went by, till at last the ruby fell from its frayed setting. He saw the ruby reset in a high carved Spanish comb. From mother to daughter he saw the comb passed down, while gradually its story was forgotten, till all its wearer knew now was that she must never lose it, or woe would come upon the world.

He saw its wearer now — a young Spanish girl, called (for she was as happy as the day is long) Senorita Serenita. He saw the ruby gleam in her smoothly piled black hair as she moved in and out of the sunlit courtyard of the little house below Mount Salvat in which she lived alone.

The wizard was a mighty shape shifter. He had only to think like any bird or beast, and he *was* that bird or beast. He thought now like a carrion crow, and he *was* a carrion crow. Away he flew, over the desert, over the sea, over the orange groves of Spain, to alight in the sunny courtyard of Senorita Serenita.

With the noon sun, sleep had stolen over all Spain. Senorita Serenita, taking her siesta in the cool shade of a leafy orange tree by the high wall of the courtyard, did not feel the wizard's bony beak draw the carved comb from her hair, did not see it peck the ruby from its setting and shut with a snap as the scrawny throat gulped it down.

Nor did she see the carrion crow hide her comb in his breast feathers, and spread wide black wings, and sweep away toward the south. But when she woke, and piled her hair afresh, and found her comb was missing, all her happiness went from her.

To and fro she ran, weeping like a fountain, wringing her hands till they bled, searching the stones of the courtyard, shaking the orange tree boughs, and all the time moaning:

"Alas, alas, Serenita! What woe will you bring on the world?"

On flew the carrion crow the rest of that day — south over the orange groves of Spain, south over the sea, then east over the desert, east over forests, east over mountains, and east over plains.

Now day was waning; now night was waxing. Still on he flew, under black sky and brilliant stars, till, just as the first cocks were crowing, he came to the eastern shore of the World's End.

Out of his dark wisdom the wizard knew that only one creature in all the world can swallow the sun: this is the wolf. At each eclipse of the sun he had watched the same drama — the sun fleeing, the world pursuing, the wolf swallowing, the world darkening. But always the sun was too mighty for the wolf, and, burning him to ashes, burst forth again in splendour.

The carrion crow thought like a wolf, and he *was* a wolf, the carved comb clinging to his shaggy pelt. Then he clad the thought of himself in iron, to meet the might of the sun with the might of that sternest of metals. He *was* an iron wolf. From his iron breast the comb fell to the sand.

As the sun came slowly up out of the sea, staining the sky with rose, the iron wolf, opening iron jaws, sprang upon him and gulped him down. The rosy sky grew grey. The birds ceased their dawn chorus between one note and the next. Twilight fell on the whole world.

Now Fosterling the Faun lived on the eastern shore of the World's End, with his foster father, a white unicorn. Just as night was waning and day was waxing he always woke, for he loved to greet his friend the sun as he rose out of the sea. But today, before he had time to greet him, his friend vanished, and day waned again.

Now a faun, as everyone knows who has ever met one, is just like any other boy except for the tiny horns among his curls. So, just as any other boy would do if his friend vanished before his eyes, he battered his foster father awake.

"Wake up, Father Unicorn!" he cried. "Friend Sun has vanished!"

Now a unicorn, as everyone knows who has ever met one, is just like any other small white horse except for the long horn growing out of his brow. This horn is so sharp that there is no substance it cannot pierce; and it gives the unicorn his power to see anything he looks for all the wide world over.

So now Father Unicorn looked for the sun; and as soon as he looked for him he found him.

"An iron wolf has eaten Friend Sun," he reported, "together with the biggest ruby in the world."

"Can we get them back?" asked Fosterling, running anxiously to and fro at the edge of the sea.

"Only with the help," said Father Unicorn, "of the owner of the ruby."

Fosterling tripped as he ran, and stooped to pick up what had tripped him. It was Senorita Serenita's comb.

"What *is* this?" he asked. "I have never seen one before."

For, as everyone knows who has ever met one, neither fauns nor unicorns as a rule wear combs in their hair.

"It is a comb, a Spanish one," Father Unicorn told him. "Ladies wear them in their hair. Look, Fosterling, there is a hole in it where a huge gem has been! If that gem was this ruby, it must have come from Spain."

As soon as he looked for Spain, he found Spain. As soon as he looked in Spain for the owner of the ruby, he found the owner of the ruby. He found her running to and fro, weeping like a fountain, wringing her hands till they bled, searching the stones of her courtyard, shaking her orange tree boughs, and all the time moaning:

"Alas, alas, Serenita! When you lost the ruby of Amfortas, what woe you brought on the world!"

"Up with you, Fosterling!" ordered Father Unicorn. "Set the comb in your curls!"

With Fosterling on his back, the comb in his yellow curls, and grey twilight all about him. Father Unicorn left behind him the eastern shore of the World's End. He left behind him the plains. He left behind him the mountains. He left behind him the forests. And at last, in the same grey twilight, he came to the edge of the desert.

"Fosterling," ordered Father Unicorn, "tear out my horn!"

"I will die first," said Fosterling.

"*Then* how will you rescue Friend Sun?" Father Unicorn asked him.

So Fosterling sadly had to.

A mist arose round Father Unicorn, and within the mist a flame. When the mist and the flame had passed, there *was* no unicorn, but instead a noble black horse with a streaming mane.

"Fosterling," said the black horse, "always obey your elders; they have lived longer than you. The scorpions in this desert sting unicorns to death, but a black horse is safe from them. Up with you, Fosterling! Take my horn in your right hand!"

With Fosterling on his back, the comb in his yellow curls, the unicorn's horn in his right hand, and grey twilight all about him, the black horse left the desert behind him and came to the edge of the sea.

"Fosterling," said the black horse, "cut off my mane!"

"I will die first," said Fosterling.

"*Then* how will you rescue Friend Sun?" the black horse asked him.

So Fosterling sadly had to.

A mist arose round the black horse, and within the mist a flame. When the mist and the flame had passed, there *was* no black horse; but Pegasus stood there, pawing the sand, his great wings beating like a butterfly's.

"Fosterling," said Pegasus, "always obey your elders; they have lived longer than you. Only a winged horse can carry you over the sea. Up with you, Fosterling! Take the black mane in your left hand!"

With Fosterling on his back, the comb in his yellow curls, the unicorn's horn in his right hand, the black horse's mane in his left, and grey twilight all about him, Pegasus left behind him the sea, left behind him the orange groves of Spain, and came to the foot of Mount Salvat.

There they found Senorita Serenita, all her happiness gone from her as she moaned beneath her orange tree:

"Alas, alas, Serenita! How can you heal this woe you have brought upon the world?"

"We are here to take you to heal it," Pegasus told her; and Fosterling took her comb from his yellow curls and held it out to her.

She set the comb in her own black locks, and mounted Pegasus behind Fosterling. With grey twilight all about them, they left behind them the orange groves; they left behind them the sea; they left behind them the desert, the forests, the mountains, the plains; they came to the eastern shore of the World's End.

"Fosterling," ordered Pegasus, "drown me!"

"I will die first," said Fosterling.

"*Then* how will you rescue Friend Sun?" Pegasus asked him.

So Fosterling sadly had to.

Under the waves sank Pegasus. A mist arose above him, and within the mist a flame. When the mist and the flame had passed, there *was* no Pegasus, but out of the waves there rose a golden eagle.

"Fosterling," said the golden eagle, "always obey your elders; they have lived longer than you. Only an eagle can look Friend Sun full in the face. Up, both of you! Bind yourselves to my back with the black horse's mane. Fosterling, give Senorita Serenita the unicorn's horn; for only she can free Friend Sun and the ruby of Amfortas."

With Fosterling and Senorita Serenita bound firmly to his back, grey twilight all about him, the golden eagle flew out to a rock in the sea, where an iron wolf crouched, howling in agony.

"Save me! Save me!" he howled. "Save me from this sun that burns and blazes in my breast!"

Senorita Serenita leaned from the golden eagle's back, with her left hand holding on to Fosterling's shoulder, in her right hand the unicorn's horn, so sharp that there was no substance it could not pierce. With it she pierced the iron wolf's breast, just where her comb had rested.

Out burst Friend Sun, so blinding bright that Fosterling and Senorita Serenita hid their eyes in the golden eagle's feathers; so blinding bright that they would have fallen with the shock of so much splendour had they not been bound in safety with the black horse's mane.

But the golden eagle stared at Friend Sun undazzled, watching for the ruby of Amfortas to follow in his wake. He caught it in his beak, just as it would have fallen into the sea. The iron wolf, breathing his last breath, howling his last howl, slid from the rock; and the waves closed over him as if he had never been.

Friend Sun began to climb the sky; the birds took up their dawn chorus just where they had left off; the grey twilight waned, and warmth and light and colour waxed till they flooded the whole world.

Back on the eastern shore, at the very spot where Fosterling had tripped over the comb, the beak of the golden eagle reset the great ruby the carrion crow's beak had pecked out.

"Fosterling," said the golden eagle, "always obey your elders; they have lived longer than you. You had better marry Senorita Serenita and help her to guard her ruby and to be as happy as the day is long again."

So Fosterling joyfully had to.

The Gorgeous Nightingale

As was usual, then as now, twelve godmothers came to the christening of the Princess Betula-Alba. One by one they came to the golden cradle with their life gifts: she would grow up gentle and kind; hers would be the graces of the silver birch tree; she would marry a youth as clear and precious as jasper.

The last godmother but one laid a tiny vial of crystal in the princess' tiny hand. It held the rainbow spark of a dewdrop. As she did so, the door burst open, and in stamped an old crone as hideous as a nightmare.

"I see the princess has the Dewdrop of Life," she croaked. "But she will only throw it away!"

And out she stamped again, banging the door behind her, so that the tapestries on the stone walls blew about with the wind of her going, while the christening guests stared at each other with eyes as big as saucers.

"She *will* throw it away," said the last godmother of all. "But in doing so she will save her father from the worst of deaths."

The queen took care of the crystal vial till Betula-Alba grew up. Then she had a golden locket made to hold it, shaped like a heart, and she hung it on a golden chain around Betula-Alba's neck, bidding her to wear the heart of gold day and night next to her own.

The very next morning Betula-Alba was wakened

early by bird song in the wood beyond the palace gardens. She left her bed and went lightly over the dewy grass to the wood. Just as the sun came over the edge of the world, broad and red and glorious, she saw a shepherd boy standing under a silver birch tree, his flock close and quiet about him.

He stood in a brown cloud of small birds, all singing their small hearts out, while out of the sky larks dropped in singing spirals to join them. The shepherd boy gazed at the princess, and the princess gazed at the shepherd boy; and she did not need to be told that his name was Jasper.

She went that morning to her father's throne room. He sat on his hard golden throne, wearing his hard golden crown.

"Father," she said, "I have found the youth as clear and precious as jasper. He is a shepherd boy."

"A shepherd boy?" thundered King Magnus. "When a nightingale is as gorgeous as a peacock, then and only then shall my daughter marry a shepherd boy!"

And he had the shepherd boy shut up in a tower with water, as far as the eye could reach, on all four sides of it.

That night, as Betula-Alba lay awake, she heard a nightingale singing. She went out into the moonlight, and stood under his bough, and told him where Jasper was, and begged him to go and sing to him, to comfort him in his loneliness.

Away flew the nightingale, over field and fell and moor and mountain, to the tower in the lake. He lit on the ivy near a slit in the thick stone wall; he sipped a drop of dew from an ivy leaf to make his throttle clear; and he lifted up his small brown throat and sang.

In his dark dungeon, Jasper stood chained to a pillar; his head was sunk on his breast, and the heart in that breast was heavy. Suddenly, rising triumphantly above the wailing of the wind and the lapping of water on stone, came the first rich notes of the song of a nightingale. Jasper lifted his head and turned his eyes to the moonlit slit, and felt his heart eased and comforted.

When the birds that greet the sun awoke and drank their drops of dew to make their throttles clear, the nightingale was still singing. From all parts of the kingdom, over field and fell and moor and mountain, his song drew them to the tower in the lake, till you could see neither stone nor ivy for small brown birds.

And as the sun came over the edge of the world, broad and red and glorious, they greeted it with such might and main that Jasper forgot his captivity, and even his warders crowded to the arrow-slits, open-mouthed, to listen.

They sent to tell King Magnus of this invasion of singing birds; and the next night he had himself rowed out to the tower in his royal barge. Again the nightingale came and sang; and again, at dawn, clouds of other birds flew to sing with him; and King Magnus thought as he listened:

"I am not *really* harsh and cruel; my true self is quite different. If I can get this nightingale to sing to *me*, all these other birds will join him; and that will *show* how gentle and kind I really am at heart."

So he had the nightingale caught and put into a golden cage; and he had the golden cage hung in his throne room. Then in he came in his royal robes and his golden crown, and, sitting on his golden throne, he barked out:

"Sing, you nightingale!"

The nightingale shrank away from the king, as far as his cage would let him. His heart beat wildly, but he did not sing one note.

"Sing, you nightingale!" King Magnus barked again.

Still the nightingale sat huddled in his corner; still he did not sing one note.

King Magnus strode to the golden cage and shook his fist in the nightingale's face.

"Sing! For the last time, sing, you nightingale!" he shouted. "Sing, or your neck shall be wrung, and you shall be plucked and roasted and served up tonight at my table!"

But the nightingale still sat huddled in his corner; and still he did not sing one note.

Then King Magnus dashed his crown on the throne-room floor, denting it rather badly, and flung open the door, and bellowed for his cook to fetch the nightingale; and the cook came and took away the nightingale in his golden cage.

Betula-Alba heard that bellow far away in the wood. She ran across the palace gardens and burst into the throne room.

"What was it, Father?" she asked. "Were you talking about *my* nightingale? Where is he?"

"In the kitchen," King Magnus snapped.

Betula-Alba flew like a bird. In the palace kitchen the golden cage stood empty, and on a roasting pan beside it, already plucked, lay the nightingale.

Betula-Alba, with a little moan, drew up the golden heart that lay on her own. She had taken out the tiny crystal vial and unscrewed its silver stopper, and was just tipping out the dewdrop, when in strode King Magnus and roughly caught her wrist.

"That dewdrop is to save *me* from death!" he stormed. "How dare you throw it away?"

"Isn't that what it was foretold I *would* do, Father?" asked Betula-Alba.

And she twisted her wrist in his iron grip, so that the Dewdrop of Life fell *splash* on the dead, naked nightingale.

Then up stood the nightingale in the roasting pan, in only his flesh and his bones; and he lifted up his stringy throat and sang. Betula-Alba swooped and cupped him in her hands; and out she ran with him, still singing, across the palace gardens to Jasper's silver birch tree.

At the call of that song, birds came flocking till you could not see Betula-Alba's golden dress for birds. Then she opened her hands and showed them the naked nightingale, and asked if each could spare him just one feather to help clothe his nakedness.

What a delicious chirping and chirruping broke out then, as each bird, preening and sleeking his feathers, called on his neighbours to help him choose his best and most beautiful one!

Now there was a flying queue to Betula-Alba's shoulder, a feather in each bird's beak. The robins brought red ones from their breasts, the chaffinches white ones from their barred wings, the golden-crested wrens yellow ones from their crowns to make a new crown for the nightingale. There were black ones from the blackbirds, blue from the jays, green from the woodpeckers, iris from the doves, and all the browns under the sun from the small brown birds like bark.

Each feather grafted itself on the nightingale's nakedness as if guided by an invisible imping needle, till Betula-Alba called joyfully to the birds:

"Bravo! You have made our little nightingale as gorgeous as a peacock!"

Her own words rang in her ears as if another's voice had said them, and at the memory they evoked, a surge of hope shook her. She hid the gorgeous nightingale in her bosom and ran back across the gardens, bursting into the throne room like a happy wind.

King Magnus was sitting on his throne in solitary state, wearing his dented crown, looking, truth to tell, a little lonely and pathetic. Betula-Alba laid a gentle hand on his arm as she asked him, her face shining:

"Father, *when* did you say I could marry Jasper?"

"When a nightingale is as gorgeous as a peacock," he snapped, "and I meant it, every word."

Betula-Alba laughed a laugh of purest joy as she drew the many-coloured nightingale from her bosom.

"That is no nightingale!" King Magnus barked, scowling at this vision of pygmy splendours. "If he is, let him sing!"

The nightingale stood up on Betula-Alba's palm. He spread out his rainbow plumage, and perkily cocked his golden feather crown at the king's golden dented one, and lifted his iridescent little throat and sang.

King Magnus nodded, knowing at once this was truly a nightingale, for the sweet pangs of a nightingale's song can melt a heart of stone. His own heart melted as he listened, so that he suddenly saw how near his own best self had come to being slain by pride and cruelty. He put his arm about Betula-Alba and drew her to him.

"Godmother Twelve was right — you have saved me from the worst of deaths," he said. "Quick, let us send for Jasper, and you shall marry him here and now!"

Every bird in the kingdom came to that wedding feast. They took crumbs of wedding cake from the lips of bride and bridegroom, and sipped hydromel (which is honey wine) to make their throttles clear, and sang as they had never sung before; but the sweetest singer of them all was the gorgeous nightingale.

And from that day King Magnus, with all the fire and force that till then he had put into being a tyrant, began to live up to his name.

New Days, New Ways

The island kingdom had only one harbour; steep cliffs, such as no man could climb, protected it everywhere else. The city built about the harbour was protected by stout sea walls. In this city the king had his palace.

In the middle of the palace was the king's room; in the middle of the king's room was the king's bed; at the head of the king's bed was the king's candle.

The king's candle was made of the purest beeswax; it stood thicker than his body; it stood taller than his head; its wick was a bunch of rushes too big to be clasped by a man's joined hands. The candle never burned away; it went out only once in the king's lifetime, and that was when that life ended.

When the king's candle went out, every light in the kingdom, every fire in the kingdom, went out with it. Then, frantically, the people came running to the palace, each with a wax taper clasped in one palm, and a copper coin clasped in the other, to buy new light, new fire, from the new king's candle. For this was the custom in those days and in that kingdom.

"The king is dead. Long live the king!" they shouted over and over again, till a clash of golden rings and silver bells told them that the new king's candle was lit.

For the king's candle was relit by a spear whose blazing head was kept in a tall jade jar filled with water. All the sons of the dead king had to pass before the candle; and as the one who was to be the next king passed, the spear sprang out of the water and lit the candle from its own blazing tip.

Strung on the spear's shaft were fifty clashing rings of gold; hung on the rings were five hundred clashing bells of silver; it was the clangour of these bells and rings as the spear came to life that rang out the glad tidings that fire and candlelight had been born anew in the land.

One day, a king of this kingdom died, leaving neither chick nor child. Out went his candle; out went every light, out went every fire, all over the island.

The people came running, a taper in one hand, a copper coin in the other. The crowd before the palace was so dense that a fly could not have edged its way between them.

The dead king's dead brother had left seven sons, so the king's wise man sent for these princes, to pass before the king's candle. One by one they passed; but still the spear stayed in a trance, its head in the jade jar of water.

"Here is a new thing!" cried the seven princes. "What does it mean?"

"It means," said the wise man, "that not one of you seven is the king."

"Does it, indeed?" raged the eldest prince, Prince Zabulo. "We will see about that!"

And he plucked forth the spear from its jar, to light the king's candle himself.

The crowds outside the palace heard the clash of golden rings and silver bells; and at once they set up a clamour:

"Long live the king!"

But no new king came out to bid them enter and light their tapers; and soon the rumour was blowing from mouth to mouth that Prince Zabulo had plucked the spear from its jar and its blazing head had gone out.

And so indeed it had; for, as he withdrew the spear's blazing head from the water, the flame at its point went out with a pop. He held the still-glowing top to the candlewick; but no candle flame sprang up.

Instead, the spear writhed out of his hand; like a giant quill guided by unseen fingers, its red tip traced four words on the marble floor before the spear fell with a clang. In letters of fire they shone out:

"New days, new ways."

The wise man and the seven princes watched the letters slowly fade. When they lifted the spear, its tip was already cold.

"Here is another new thing!" cried the princes. "With no spear, how shall we choose which one of us is to be king?"

"Not one of you is to be king," the wise man replied. "New days, new ways."

And he sent heralds by swift boat to all the nearby kingdoms, to proclaim that the first prince of any land to light the king's candle should be king of this land.

From every point of the compass, royal ships came bearing down upon the island's harbour — galleys with gilded poops, longships with dragon prows, galleons, caravels, sashmarays. (For all this took place some time ago, when we were younger than we are today.)

The ships were laden with lighted lamps and lanterns, with fire in braziers, buckets, boxes, and even warming pans. But the moment the princes brought them ashore on the island, every light, every fire, shot out a spark and went out.

"Here is yet another new thing!" observed the seven princes, well pleased. "Old fire will not live in our land."

But the people, who had no fires to cook their suppers and who had to go to bed these days as soon as it was dark, were not so pleased.

"A king! A king!" they roared. "Give us a new king, you wise man and you princes, or we will empty your eight bodies of your souls!"

So the wise man sent heralds by swift boat again, to proclaim that if *any* fire-maker could make new fire on the island and light the king's candle with it, he should be king, even though he had not one drop of royal blood in his body.

For, with the king's candle always there, nobody in the whole island had the least notion as to how to make new fire; and in those days matches had not yet been invented, much less cigarette lighters.

Three days later, the watchmen on the sea walls sent word to the palace that a boat approached. The wise man came in haste, with the seven princes at his heels, and with all the people at theirs. They saw a stranger, as tall and thin as a hop-pole, paddling a bark canoe into the harbour. He was wrapped in a bright blanket, and he wore dyed feathers in his hair.

"What will you make new fire with?" the wise man asked him.

"With these," said the stranger. From beneath his blanket he brought out a cylinder like a sharpened pencil and a block of wood with a cup-shaped hollow in it. "What are the king's dues here for new light?"

"A copper coin from each roof tree," the wise man told him.

"To me they shall pay a silver one," said the stranger.

The people groaned. But light they must have, and

fire they must have; so they parted for the stranger to pass between them to the palace.

In the king's room, the stranger asked the wise man to hold the block of wood steady for him. Into the hollow he set the sharpened point of his borer, and twirled till the wood grew hot and a languid wing of transparent flame shot up.

The princes drew in their breaths sharply, but the flame died as soon as it was born; and twirl as the stranger would, no further fire could he make.

"This works in my own land," said the stranger, much perplexed. "It may be that to work here, it needs wood grown in this kingdom."

The wise man looked close at both borer and cup.

"We grow no wood on our island as hard as your drill," he said, "and no wood as soft as your matrix."

So the man with the fire drill paddled his bark canoe sadly away; and the king's candle still stood unlit.

Next day, the watchmen on the sea walls sent word to the palace that a second boat approached. The wise man came in haste, with the seven princes at his heels, and with all the people at theirs. They saw a stranger, as four-square as a tower, rowing a coracle of wicker and hides into the harbour.

A silver shoulder-brooch held the folds of his plaid in place, and at the front of his tartan kilt hung a goatskin sporran.

"What will you make new fire with?" the wise man asked him.

"With these," said the stranger, and out of his sporran he took a flint and a meteorite. "What are the king's dues here for a new light?"

"A copper coin from each roof tree," the wise man told him.

"To me they shall pay a gold one," said the stranger.

The people groaned. But light they must have, and fire they must have; so they parted for the stranger to pass between them to the palace.

In the king's room, the stranger struck earthly stone and heavenly stone together. A spark leaped forth.

The princes drew in their breaths sharply. But the spark died before it fell on the tinder placed to receive it; and strike stone on stone as the stranger would, no further spark was born.

"This works in my own land," said the stranger, much perplexed. "It may be that to work here, it needs flint from your own rocks, and star iron that has fallen into your own fields."

The wise man looked close at both flint and meteorite.

"We have neither of these on our island," he said.

So the stranger put flint and meteorite back into his sporran, and rowed his hide coracle sadly away; and the king's candle stood unlit.

It was still before sunrise next day when the watchmen on the sea walls were roused by a hail from the water, and a cheerful young voice asking for leave to land.

"Can you not wait to begin your day with the sun, as other men do?" they grumbled.

"The sun and my boat are so drawn to each other," the happy young voice replied, "that I dare only sail her by night."

They gave him leave to land. Still in the dark before dawn, he shrouded the boat in its sail and begged one of the watchmen to guard it with his life.

"For there is not such another in all the seven seas," he said.

"You made it with your own hands?" the watchmen asked.

"And my own mouth," the stranger added.

At sunrise the wise man came in haste, with the seven princes at his heels, and with all the people at theirs. The stranger they came to greet was a youth, barefoot and in rags, his lips twitching with laughter at the jests he was telling himself.

"What will you make new fire with?" the wise man asked him.

"With this," said the stranger. Out of his rags he drew a transparent, colourless globe, a little like a crystal.

"And what king's dues will *you* charge for new light?" asked a voice from the dense crowd.

"Gutrin's candlelight shall be as free as sunlight," answered Gutrin.

The crowd cheered; they shouted words of friendship as they made a lane for him to the palace.

In the king's room, Gutrin opened the horn casement wide and had the king's candle set near it. In the sunlight that came pouring in, he held up his colourless sphere, standing as still as a stone.

All eyes were fixed on the sphere as the sunlight streamed into it. But suddenly the wise man gave a cry: "The king's candle! The candle is lit!"

The glad tidings swept like wildfire through the palace and out to the waiting people. A roar of joy went up from them like the roaring of the sea. They battered open the palace doors; and in they surged, tapers in hand, for their free candlelight.

But the seven princes swept Gutrin, and the wise man with him, into the king's robing chamber; and their voices were as shrill as cats in the moonlight as they shrieked:

"But he did nothing — nothing! Is he to be king for merely holding a jewel in the sun?"

"Unless the sun light the candle," answered Gutrin, still smiling, "a man labours in vain to light it."

"But how did the jewel do it?" shrieked the princes.

They snatched the globe from him to see. They snatched it from one another. All in a flash, no one quite knew how, *crash* it fell on the marble floor.

They drew apart. The transparent globe lay splintered into tiny fragments. About the fragments spread a tiny pool.

"Then it was *not* a jewel!" Prince Zabulo accused him.

"*You* called it that, not I," smiled Gutrin. "It was a hollow sphere of glass."

"Glass? What is glass?" asked the wise man.

"A substance you can see through, made from sand," Gutrin told him. "That is how I got my name; Gutrin means glass. You see, I am a glass blower."

"Sand," mused the wise man. "We have no sand on our island. And what was the liquid in the globe?"

"Water," said Gutrin.

"Water?" howled Prince Zabulo. "You won my uncle's throne with sand and water? No, that is too much. My sword slips very easily from its scabbard. What is to stop it from slipping now and leaving you a head shorter?"

"This," said the wise man sternly, "that when a king is every poor man's friend, every poor man is his. Touch a hair of your new king's head, and the people will tear you to tatters."

The sound of a horn smote them all into sudden silence. A breathless messenger entered and knelt before the new king, the king still in his rags.

"Sire, the watchmen on the sea walls have sighted an armada," he announced. "It sails toward our harbour. It is the war fleet of the king who tried last year to take our land."

"He thinks to take it easily now with, as he thinks, no king's candle alight," said the wise man. "Sire, you must ring the war alarm and man the walls!"

"No," said King Gutrin suddenly. "He has come on a day of bright sun; that has delivered him into our hands. We can defeat that armada without the loss of one man."

He ran down to the harbour, wise man and princes at his heels, the people at theirs. He drew the sail from his shrouded boat, and they saw it was a boat of glass, as clear and as round as a goldfish bowl.

"Fill it with water," commanded King Gutrin.

The people ran to do his bidding.

"Now set up the crane for casting stones at the foe," he commanded again. "Set it up in the place I will show you. Then set my boat in it and lift it high."

And again the people ran to do his bidding.

"Leave the walls unmanned," he ordered.

And they did so.

On came the war fleet; it cast anchor just out of bowshot of the walls. The walls were deserted. No army was gathered; no ships were manned. Only a great transparent globe hung high in the air. The invading king feared a trap and sent to consult his leaders.

While they argued this way and that, the sunlight streamed into the great glass globe of water. Powerfully it focused the sun's rays upon the wooden ships. Soon smoke began to rise, then flames to leap and lap and spread. The armada was on fire.

As King Gutrin had foretold, he defeated the invaders without the loss of one man.

When the last charred and crippled ship had limped

away over the skyline, King Gutrin, still in rags, turned to go back to the palace.

"Long live the king!" roared the people, pressing about him.

"Long live the king!" echoed the princes, changed from foes to friends.

And live long he did, the friend of all in that country.

Rose-Child and Lily-Child

The king's twin sons were as much alike as two peas in a pod. When one fell sick, they both fell sick.

The royal physicians racked their brains and their pharmacopoeias, but nothing they found in either could cure the royal twins.

"Your Majesty," said the Chief Royal Physician at last, "what did you lose just before the princes fell sick?"

"Lose?" repeated the king, slapping all the pockets in his royal robes. "Why, bless my soul, I remember now — I lost my little-finger ring."

"I thought as much," nodded the Chief Royal Physician. "It has come into the Witch-Queen's hands and given her power over the princes. They will never be well again until you get it back."

The king promised fountains of jewels, and gold in a solid shower, to anyone who would bring him back his little-finger ring. But though many set out to fetch it, no one brought it back; for in her own land the Witch-Queen had power over earth and fire and water, and all the ways to her castle were strewn with strong enchantments.

Now the king's gardener had twin daughters, Rose-Child and Lily-Child.

"Lily-Child," said Rose-Child, "I am going to fetch that

ring. Watch my rosebush while I am gone. If its flowers stay fresh, things will be well with me; if they droop, things will be ill with me."

Off she set, over the green meadows. Though the grass was green, it grew greener where she trod; and in every footprint grew a rose the size of a little-finger ring, in every footprint grew a small red rose.

She went a short way, she went a long way, and she came to a stream. A fish lay gasping on its bank. She put him back into the stream; and on she went.

She went a short way, she went a long way, and she came to a mill. An otter was whirling in the millrace. She helped him back to land; and on she went.

She went a short way, she went a long way, and she came to a wild water. There was no bridge. There was no boat.

"What of it?" said Rose-Child. "I can swim."

But as soon as she twiddled her toes in the water, she vanished in a puff of smoke.

At that very moment, in the garden at home, Rose-Child's rose tree began to wilt.

"*Now* where has Rose-Child got to?" said Lily-Child.

Off she set to find her, over the green meadows, following Rose-Child's footprints, in every footprint a rose the size of a little-finger ring, in every footprint a small red rose.

She went a short way, she went a long way, she came to the stream; she came to the mill; she came to the wild water. The green footprints led right down into the water, in every footprint a rose the size of a little-finger ring, in every footprint a small red rose.

The sun was overhead. Lily-Child lifted her arms, calling aloud:

"All creatures, be they bird or beast,
The greatest creature, or the least,
To whom my sister has been kind,
Help me now Rose-Child to find."

The fish came swimming. The otter came running.

"I will find her," said the fish.

He swam to a quiet backwater, and listened to the secrets in the whispering of the waters. Soon he swam back.

"I have found her," he said. "She is a white stone among the other white stones on the bed of the wild water, but out of her grows a rose the size of a little-finger ring, out of her grows a small red rose."

"I will fetch her," said the otter.

In he dived; a string of bubbles rose. Out he came, and shook himself, and laid a white stone and a small red rose at Lily-Child's feet. As soon as they touched the grass, they vanished in a puff of smoke; and there on that spot stood Rose-Child.

"Come home with me, Rose-Child," begged Lily-Child.

"I have braved one peril; I can brave two," Rose-Child replied. "Now you have broken the spell of the wild water, I can cross it without harm."

Rose-Child kissed Lily-Child. Lily-Child kissed Rose-Child. Home went Lily-Child. On went Rose-Child.

Now that the spell was broken, Rose-Child swam the wild water without harm. On the far shore she went a short way, she went a long way, and in every footprint grew a rose the size of a little-finger ring, in every footprint grew a small red rose.

She came to a butterfly caught in a spider's web. She set her free; and on she went.

She went a short way, she went a long way, and she

came to a lizard fast in a snare of clay. She set him free; and on she went.

She went a short way, she went a long way, and she came to the flaming hollow. There was no way over it. There was no way under it.

"What of it?" said Rose-Child. "I can run."

But as soon as she blew the flames apart, she vanished in a puff of smoke.

At that very moment, in the garden at home, Rose-Child's rose tree wilted again.

"*Now* where has Rose-Child got to?" said Lily-Child.

Off she sped to find her, over the green meadows, past the stream, past the mill, to the shore of the wild water.

Lily-Child lifted her arms, calling aloud:

"Wind, Wind, warm and mild,
Bear me over the water wild,
To find Rose-Child."

The wind came. The wind lifted her. The wind bore her above the wild water and set her down gently on the other side.

She went a short way, she went a long way, following Rose-Child's footprints. They led her right to the edge of the flaming hollow, in every footprint a rose the size of a little-finger ring, in every footprint a small red rose.

The sun was going down the sky. Lily-Child lifted her arms, calling aloud:

"All creatures, be they bird or beast,
The greatest creature, or the least,
To whom my sister has been kind,
Help me now Rose-Child to find."

The lizard came. The butterfly came looping the loop. "I will find her," said the butterfly.

She fluttered above the flaming hollow, listening to the secrets in the crackling of the flames. Soon she flew back.

"I have found her," she said. "She is a red stone among the other red stones that pave the flaming hollow; but out of her grows a rose the size of a little-finger ring, out of her grows a small red rose."

"I will fetch her," said the lizard. (He was a fire lizard, a salamander.)

Into the fire he darted. Out of the fire he darted. He laid a red stone and a small red rose at Lily-Child's feet. As soon as they touched the grass, they vanished in a puff of smoke; and there on that spot stood Rose-Child.

"Come home with me, Rose-Child," begged Lily-Child.

"I have braved two perils; I can brave three," Rose-Child replied. "Now you have broken the spell of the flaming hollow, I can cross it without harm."

Rose-Child kissed Lily-Child. Lily-Child kissed Rose-Child. Home went Lily-Child. On went Rose-Child.

Now that the spell was broken, Rose-Child ran through the flames without harm. On the far side, she went a short way, she went a long way, and in every footprint grew a rose the size of a little-finger ring, in every footprint grew a small red rose.

She came to a humming-bird caught in a bird net. She set her free; and on she went.

She went a short way, she went a long way, and she came to a bumble-bee caught in a treacle trap. She set her free; and on she went.

She went a short way, she went a long way, and she came to a field mouse caught in a box trap. She set him free; and on she went.

She went a short way, she went a long way, and she came to the Witch-Queen's rock garden. If there was one acre of it, there were forty; and every square inch of those forty acres was a bare black stone.

The Witch-Queen was sitting in the middle of it. She was a sight to make young blood run cold. Her teeth were as long as your fingers, her nails were as long and yellow as a kite's claw; she could crack a nut between her nose and her chin.

She had been spinning, and she had fallen asleep with her spindle on her lap. Her left hand hung down by her side; and on her middle finger (for it was too big for any other) gleamed and glowed and glittered the king's little-finger ring.

Rose-Child crept close on tiptoe and began gently to draw the ring from the Witch-Queen's finger. But the finger cried out:

"Witch-Queen, wake,
For my gold ring's sake!"

The Witch-Queen woke. At the sight of Rose-Child she showed her long teeth in wicked glee and rapped her knuckles with her spindle. Rose-Child vanished in a puff of smoke, and a new black stone fell with a clang and a clatter amid those forty acres of old ones.

The Witch-Queen sat and stared at the new black stone with wicked eyes. Presently out of it grew a rose the size of a little-finger ring; out of it grew a small red rose. The Witch-Queen tore it off.

A second rose grew in its place. The Witch-Queen tore off the second one. A third rose grew.

This rose the Witch-Queen left. She waved her spindle; and out of every bare black stone in those forty acres of rock garden grew a rose the size of a little-finger ring; out of every stone grew a small red rose.

"Puzzle find the true one," chortled the Witch-Queen; and she stood up like a tall black bat and stalked into her tall black castle for supper.

At that very moment, in the garden at home, Rose-Child's rose tree wilted a third time.

"*Now* where has Rose-Child got to?" said Lily-Child.

Off she set to find her, over the green meadows, past the stream, past the mill, to the shore of the wild water.

Lily-Child lifted her arms, calling aloud:

"Wind, Wind, warm and mild,
Bear me over the water wild,
To find Rose-Child."

The wind came. The wind lifted her. The wind bore her above the wild water, and set her down gently on the other side.

She went a short way, she went a long way, and she came to the flaming hollow. She lifted her arms, calling aloud:

"Wind, Wind, swift as a swallow,
Bear me over the flaming hollow,
Rose-Child to follow."

The wind came. The wind lifted her. The wind bore her above the flaming hollow and set her down gently on the other side.

She went a short way, she went a long way, following Rose-Child's footprints. They led her to the Witch-Queen's rock garden. Out of every stone in that forty acres grew a rose the size of a little-finger ring; out of every stone grew a small red rose.

The sun was setting. Lily-Child lifted her arms, calling aloud:

"All creatures, be they bird or beast,
The greatest creature, or the least,
To whom my sister has been kind,
Help me Rose-Child to find."

The field mouse came scuttling. The humming-bird came humming. The bumble-bee came bumbling.

"I will find her," said the bumble-bee.

She preened her wings with her front legs; then away she flew.

She bumbled from black stone to black stone, from small red rose to small red rose, all over all those forty acres of rock garden. Soon she bumbled back.

"I have found her," she buzzed. "Only one red rose in all these forty acres has scent and nectar in it."

She led Lily-Child to the true red rose. Lily-Child lifted the stone. It vanished in a puff of smoke; and there stood Rose-Child.

"Wait for me, Lily-Child," she said. "I have braved three perils; I can brave four. I am going into the castle for the ring while the Witch-Queen sleeps tonight. Her finger will not waken her again, now that the spell is broken."

"Wait yourself, Rose-Child," hummed the humming-bird.

She flew into the castle and listened to the secrets of the humming, strumming, weaving, heaving thoughts in the Witch-Queen's mind. Soon she flew back.

"The Witch-Queen is just off to bed," she told them.

"She is going to keep the king's ring under her tongue while she sleeps. She has put a spell on the castle gateway, on each step of the corkscrew staircase, and on the door-stone of her chamber, so that they will all cry out and wake her if Rose-Child tries to enter."

"Rustling cornstalks!" squeaked the field mouse. "Does she think that is the *only* way into her castle? Stay here, Rose-Child. I will scamper up the ivy and get you the ring myself. Come with me, Humming-bird, to bring it back; for the Witch-Queen has no power over anything in the air."

By now night had fallen, and the moon was coming up. The Witch-Queen's castle stood up gaunt and black against the silver sky, with only the flicker of a candle to mark the Witch-Queen's chamber.

The field mouse scampered across the forty acres of rock garden to the steep stone wall of the castle, the humming-bird flying at his tail-tip. He scampered up the ivy to the narrow slit that served the Witch-Queen as a window, and the humming-bird folded her small wings beside him on its ledge.

The slit was a tight fit even for a field mouse and a humming-bird to squeeze through; but they tucked in their waists and made themselves thin, and they just did it.

They could hear the Witch-Queen snoring and snorting in her sleep.

"Bristling barley beards!" squeaked the field mouse. "That ring is choking her!"

He ran lightly down the wall hangings to the floor, and as lightly up the bed hangings to the pillow. With the tip of his tail he tickled the Witch-Queen's nose.

"*Atishoo!*" she sneezed in her sleep, with a sound like tearing calico. The ring jumped out of her mouth with the sneeze. The humming-bird caught it in midair; out through the slit she slipped and flew across the forty acres of nectarless roses to Rose-Child, and set it on her thumb.

Then Lily-Child lifted her arms, calling softly:

"Wind, Wind, turn you round.
Bear us home to happier ground.
The ring is found!"

While the Witch-Queen was still groping blindly in her blankets for the ring, the wind came and lifted Rose-Child and Lily-Child, and bore them back in the moonlight, a short way, a long way, over flaming hollow, over wild water, past the mill, past the stream, over the sleeping meadows, and set them down safely at the gate of their own king's castle.

The king was nodding in the sickroom when Rose-Child and Lily-Child were brought in to him.

"Why, bless my soul, what's this?" he cried, as Rose-Child laid the ring in his hand.

He slipped it on his little finger, and the instant it snuggled down where it belonged, the two sick princes sat up in their beds, as strong as horses and as right as rain. They stared at Rose-Child and Lily-Child as if they thought them two angels straight from heaven; and Rose-Child and Lily-Child stared back as if they thought them the same.

"You had better get up, my boys," said the king, "and we will have a double wedding!"

And up they both got like a flash.

The Terrible Tanterabogus

The Princess Lunette could not bear the sight of the prince whom her father had said she must marry.

"If he had claws and horns and tusks and a snout and a tail," she wailed, "I could not find him uglier; and marry him I will *not*."

"Lock her in her room till she takes that back," the king told her old nurse, "and put her on dry bread and water."

"And take care the Terrible Tanterabogus does not get you," the old nurse warned the weeping princess as she dragged her out of the angry king's presence.

The Terrible Tanterabogus was the bogeyman who in that country ate bad children.

"I am not a child any longer, to be afraid of that old bogeyman," muttered Lunette, pushing out her lower lip and wiping her eyes on her long golden hair.

But she *was* still afraid of him, all the same.

All the rest of that day she was locked in her room, and fed only on dry bread and water; and that night her old nurse slept in the room, with her bed across the door, and its key safe under her pillow.

"Trouble is always to be had for the asking," sighed Lunette. "*Now* what shall I do? If I stay and give in, that ugly prince will get me. If I stay and *don't* give in, the

Terrible Tanterabogus will get me. I had better not stay at all."

There were pots of poppy plants growing in her room, covered with red and white poppies. Next day, when she was locked in alone, Lunette squeezed the juice out of some of them into a small crystal flask. At dusk, when the old nurse came in with her own savoury supper and Lunette's bread and water, Lunette cried out:

"Oh, look, Nurse! A bat at the window!"

Now the old nurse could bear bats no more than Lunette could bear the ugly prince; so away to the window she stumped, to close it with a bang. And while her back was turned, Lunette tipped the poppy juice into her soup.

Now poppy juice makes you sleep; and *how* that old nurse slept that night!

She slept while Lunette put on her jewelled sandals with soles of cork that made her footsteps as silent as a cat's.

She slept while Lunette tied tightly in a scarf the money she was given to throw among the people when she rode out in the city.

She slept while Lunette drew the key from under her pillow, crawled under her bed to the door, unlocked it, slipped through, locked it again from outside, and dropped the key into a pot of lilies in the palace corridor.

She slept while Lunette dressed herself in green hunting tunic and hose from the pages' wardrobe, and twisted up her long golden hair under a page's green cap with a feather to match.

And still that old nurse slept while Lunette stole like a cat down the corkscrew stairs, wriggled through an open grille in the venison chamber, dropped lightly onto the outside grass, and set out on her journey into the wide world.

Away loped Lunette on her soles of cork, as silent as a shadow in the moonlight, till she came to a poor man's hut on the bank of a river. Below it, on the water, tossed his boat, moored to a tree.

"Mine be yours, yours be mine!" murmured Lunette, at the sleeping man's window.

She laid the scarf filled with money on the poor man's doorstep, scrambled into his boat and untied the rope. The current was swift and strong; like an arrow loosed from a bow, away sped the boat down the river.

Far she went, far, and far farther than far. The moon went in; and there crouched Lunette in the darkness, longing for daybreak, and telling herself:

"Trouble is always to be had for the asking. *Now* what shall I do? The river has got me now. But rather the river than that awful prince or the Terrible Tanterabogus!"

Daybreak came. The river grew wilder, for a cloudburst had swollen its headwaters which now rushed seaward, crested with foam, lifting Lunette's boat high, and crashing it into a tangle of tree roots under the bank. As it tossed there, Lunette saw a small furry creature washed out of the crumbling bank, saw two tiny paws lifted like praying hands out of the spray and heard a faint, plaintive cry for help.

"Mine be yours, yours be mine!" called Lunette to the river.

She kicked off her left jewelled sandal to buy the struggling little life; the river seized it and whirled it away, bobbing like a toy cork boat. The rope that had moored her own boat she threw out as a lifeline and drew it in with a half drowned mole clinging limply to it.

"King Moldiwarp thanks you straight from his heart," said the mole, bowing, then straightened the tiny gold crown on his tiny sleek head. "Shall we step on dry land while we can?"

Lunette moored the boat to a tree root. Across the writhing roots they scrambled ashore.

"Madam," said King Moldiwarp (for you can't bamboozle a mole with a page's tunic and hose), "all the moles in my kingdom are at your service. If ever you need help, think of me, and I will be with you."

So, exchanging courtly bows, they parted.

Lunette stumbled on through a wood, left foot shoeless, right foot shod, till she came to a hollow tree, with bees flying in and out of it. From within the tree came the saddest bee-music she had ever heard; so she asked a worker bee alighting with her load:

"Why do you all sing so sadly?"

"When our hearts are sad, shall not our song be sad?" the bee replied. "We are sad because we lose our eggs as fast as our queen can lay them. For every day, along comes a bear who puts in his paw and breaks off a chunk of honeycomb to eat, and cells full of young brood with it."

"I can make it so that he couldn't," Lunette told her.

She got damp clay, and with it she built up the hole in the tree till it was just a slit big enough for bees to pass in and out, but too small for a bear's paw to go through. As it grew dry and hard, out flew the roly-poly queen, her five eyes popping with joy below her tiny gold crown.

"Madam," she said (for you can't bamboozle a bee with a page's tunic and hose), "Queen Melissa thanks you straight from her heart. All the bees in my kingdom are at your service. If ever you need help, think of me, and I will be with you."

So, exchanging courtly bows, they parted.

Lunette limped on, left foot shoeless, right foot shod, till, when the sun was high, she came out of the wood, and saw before her a ruined temple in a shady garden. By now she was hungry and thirsty as well as tired; so, sitting down in the shadow of the temple, she ate her fill of the juicy berries growing here. Then, leaning against a tree trunk, she went fast asleep.

Now the royal city of that kingdom was not far off, and it was filled with weeping and wailing. For early that morning, a messenger had ridden in, swaying in his saddle with fatigue.

"Sirs," he said to the king's counsellors, all aged men with long white beards, "the battle is lost and King Zygmund is taken prisoner. Our foes have taken the fortress guarding the river mouth, and tomorrow they will ride to take this city, also."

The old men plucked at their long white beards.

"*Now* what shall we do?" they cried. "We must send and ask the oracle." So they sent and asked the oracle.

This was the answer the oracle sent back:

"One who sleeps today at noon,
Right foot shod, and left foot bare,
Beside the Temple of the Moon,
From its foes shall free your land,
And sit upon your king's right hand,
And with him throne and kingdom share."

Swiftly and gladly then the old men called for horses; swiftly and gladly they rode out to the ruined Temple of the Moon. There, in its shadow, Lunette was wakened by the ring of hoofs and the tinkle of bridle-bells and opened her eyes to see a circle of long white beards wagging round her.

"Never was a stranger so welcome, sir!" they greeted her (for, not being moles or bees, they *were* bamboozled by the page's tunic and hose). "By what august name may we address you?"

"I must tell them a fierce one," thought Lunette, "so that they will never guess I am a runaway princess in disguise."

So, making her voice as manly and gruff as she could, she told them:

"The Terrible Tanterabogus."

The whitebeards brushed the ground as they bowed, for the name impressed them tremendously.

"And from whence has Lord Terrible Tanterabogus come to us?" they asked.

"From far, and far, and far farther than far," replied the Terrible Tanterabogus.

They mounted her on a steed (to her great comfort), and conducted her with joy to the royal palace. And there they told her what the oracle had told them.

Lunette's heart sank with a bump. But she managed to reply, in her Tanterabogus voice:

"Leave me alone now, my lords, to consider my strategy."

Joyfully they bowed and withdrew.

"Trouble is always to be had for the asking," Lunette moaned then. "*Now* what shall I do?"

She thought of Queen Melissa, and at once the roly-poly queen bee was with her, her five eyes popping with interest under her tiny golden crown as Lunette told her story.

"Madam," said Queen Melissa, "get some riding boots

made tonight; and, early tomorrow morning, ride out alone to meet the foe. Leave all the rest to me."

The royal cordwainers toiled all night to make the Terrible Tanterabogus a pair of riding boots; and early next morning Lunette put them on (slipping her jewelled sandal into the wide sleeve of her page's tunic) and rode out alone to meet the foe.

Afar across the plain she saw a great army advancing, the morning sunlight glinting on rank beyond rank of burnished helmets and coats of mail. Then suddenly she saw the ordered ranks break into wild confusion; steeds reared; riders were thrown and trampled; and mules who drew the cannons plunged and turned tail; the oxen who drew the baggage trains went berserk; and elephants who drew the battering rams ran amok.

Every bee in the kingdom flew that morning in Lunette's service. Swarm after swarm after swarm swooped to attack. The enemy were stung, and stung, and stung again, till at last they wheeled and fled; they were stung as they galloped across the plain to the shore; they were stung as they boarded their ships in panic, and, in panic, put out to sea.

Lunette, sitting on her horse on the cliff top, watched their sails grow small on the skyline; then rode quietly back to a city whose every roof was raised with the praises of the Terrible Tanterabogus.

"Sleep now, Lord Terrible Tanterabogus," the whitebeards begged her, "that tomorrow you may take the fortress our foes still hold and set King Zygmund free."

Joyfully they bowed and withdrew.

"Trouble is always to be had for the asking," Lunette sighed then. "*Now* what shall I do?"

She thought of King Moldiwarp, and at once he was

with her in his sleek fur coat, his tiny gold crown tipped over his long nose as he listened to her story.

"Madam," he said, "lead what is left of King Zygmund's army to the fortress tomorrow. Go dressed as a herald, and proclaim the message I will give you. Leave all the rest to me."

Early next morning Lunette rode out, at the head of her army, to the fortress guarding the river mouth. She wore a herald's tabard over her hunting tunic; a herald's trumpet was slung across her chest.

At the fortress gate she sounded her herald's trumpet, and proclaimed to the warders in her Tanterabogus voice:

"The Terrible Tanterabogus gives you till noon to deliver King Zygmund to him unharmed and leave the fortress. Already its walls are being undermined. Come to them half an hour before noon; and what you will see will make your hair stand on end."

The warders laughed her to scorn; but half an hour before noon the walls were so thronged with soldiers that you could not have dropped a stone among them.

They looked right; they looked left; they looked up; they looked down; but nowhere could they see anything new but the herald quietly sitting his horse, and, behind him, the ranks of his army. Jeers broke out:

"You have not lifted a single hair on our heads yet, Terrible Tanterabogus!"

But suddenly across the jeers struck a voice shrill with alarm:

"Look! Look! The ground is heaving!"

And now from the whole ring of the city's walls the same cry rose:

"Look! Look! The ground is heaving!"

Every mole in the kingdom was toiling underground

that day in Lunette's service. Moles come to the surface at eight, at noon, and at four, King Moldiwarp had told her; each time, the soil would heave for half an hour before they threw up their molehills. Seen from above, that circle of heaving earth was so sinister that the hair of the watchers really did stand on end with their terror. The gates were opened; the keys were delivered to the herald; the captive King Zygmund rode forth unharmed; the enemy garrison marched out in haste, boarded their ships and scuttled away; the home garrison marched in.

When Lunette had kicked off her jewelled sandal into the river to buy King Moldiwarp's life, its cork sole had kept it afloat as the current whirled it away. A mouse, swept from the bank by an ebbing wave, had been catapulted right into it, and was borne by it on down the river as far as the river mouth. Here it was caught up in a crosscurrent, which cast it against the wall of the fortress again and again, just beneath the barred grille of a dungeon.

In this very dungeon young King Zygmund had been imprisoned. Peering out, he had been aware of the river rising till now and again a wave washed in at his grille. When now he saw the flash of jewels spinning back and forth in the water, he put out his hand between the bars, groped, waited, pounced, and drew the sandal in.

Out sprang the mouse who sat up on the dungeon floor, wiped his whiskers, folded his paws, and bowed with extreme politeness.

"Sir, my name is Souris," he said. (He was a French mouse.) "Sir, I owe you my life. If, sir, the help of a common house mouse with a taste for travel is ever of any use to you, mine is at your service any hour of the day or night."

King Zygmund thanked him gravely; but all the while

he could not tear his gaze from the sandal in his hand. It was so delicate and dainty, so foolish yet so brave, that there and then he fell head over heels in love with the delicate, dainty, brave and foolish lady who had worn it.

"Have you travelled far, my friend?" he asked craftily.

"Far, and far, and far farther than far," Souris told him.

"And all the way in your jewelled boat?" asked King Zygmund.

"No, sir, only the last lap of my journey," Souris replied. "Dry land gave way under me; the river offered me this boat, and — *voila!* Pray, sir, how do you yourself come to be here?"

King Zygmund told him.

"Then, sir," said Souris, "I will stay here with you, and run about the fortress and pick you up crumbs of information."

"I have only crumbs of dry bread to offer you in return, my friend," King Zygmund warned him.

"*Zut!* Who cares?" said Souris. "A mouse with a taste for travel is glad of what he gets."

He dressed his whiskers and scuttled away. Presently he was back, his beady eyes gleaming.

"Sir, your whitebeards have found a champion," he announced. "He is the Terrible Tanterabogus, and the oracle says he will free you and share your throne and kingdom."

"Who *is* the Terrible Tanterabogus?" King Zygmund asked, astonished at this news.

"Sir, in one land I passed through," Souris told him, "I gathered he is a bogeyman who eats bad children."

"Share my throne with a child-eating bogeyman?" exclaimed King Zygmund, horrified. "My whitebeards must be in their dotage to believe the oracle foretold *that!*"

Next evening, Souris came scampering in, his whiskers bristling with excitement.

"Sir, the Terrible Tanterabogus is outside the fortress with an army, and he says you will be free by noon!"

And again, just before noon:

"Quick, quick, King Zygmund! Let me leap into your sleeve! They are coming to release you!"

A key turned rustily in the lock. King Zygmund was led along dark passages, up stairs in the thickness of the fortress walls, and out into clear daylight. He was mounted on a horse; the gates were opened; and forth from his prison he rode free, to meet the Terrible Tanterabogus.

Anything less like a child-eating bogeyman than the Terrible Tanterabogus King Zygmund could not imagine. To share throne and kingdom with this beautiful youth would be the greatest pleasure he could think of.

They rode back to the royal city over ways strewn with flowers, each finding joy in the other's company. When they sat side by side in the throne room, and the whitebeards and the courtiers withdrew, King Zygmund whispered:

"And now, Terrible Tanterabogus, to mark my deep gratitude, I am going to show you my most precious possession!"

And from his left sleeve he drew out the jewelled sandal.

To his astonishment, the Terrible Tanterabogus snatched it from him, and was away like a hare down the length of the throne room. Away like a hound went King Zygmund in pursuit, and caught the Terrible Tanterabogus at the door.

"Give me back my sandal, Terrible Tanterabogus," he pleaded. "It is more to me than my life."

"It was mine before it was yours!" cried Lunette; and in her excitement she quite forgot to use her Tanterabogus voice. "Pull off my riding boots, and you shall see!"

She sat on the throne again, and King Zygmund drew off her riding boots. She slipped her left foot into his sandal, and it fitted like a glove. Then out of her own sleeve she took its fellow, and slipped her right foot into that. There could not be the least doubt in the world that these sandals had been made for her.

"But if that is so," thought King Zygmund in despair, "the lady I love just *isn't*!"

Then in his mind's eye he saw again the Terrible Tanterabogus running down the throne room.

"The Terrible Tanterabogus runs like a girl," he thought. "And now I come to think of it, he walks like a girl; and, when he forgets, he talks like a girl; he has a girl's small feet, and a girl's small waist. My eyes and my ears and my heart all tell me he is a girl. How can I make sure?"

He shook his right sleeve, and out sprang Souris, scampering about the room, scratching and scrabbling the floor with his feet so that the Terrible Tanterabogus would hear him.

The Terrible Tanterabogus heard him. The Terrible Tanterabogus saw him. The Terrible Tanterabogus gave a shriek that rang all round the throne room, all round the palace, all round the city. Only a girl could have given such a shriek.

The Terrible Tanterabogus sprang high in the air and landed on the throne, hands pressed to knees as if tightly clutching long skirts.

The canopy of the throne knocked the page's cap from the head of the Terrible Tanterabogus; and down tumbled lock after lock of knee-long golden hair.

"O Terrible Tanterabogus, will you marry me," asked King Zygmund, all alight with laughter, "and really share my throne and kingdom?"

He came to her with arms lifted; and this time there was no need for him to catch her.

Cocorico and Coquelicot

The farm cocks were crowing the world awake when the farmer's son was born; so they called him Cocorico.

Cocorico could crow before he could talk. He could cockstride before he could walk. Even his hair stuck up in drakes' tails and cocks' feathers. And from the moment he could crawl, he went out every morning before breakfast, to pass the time of day with Roo, the farmyard's feathered father.

Cocks are knowing birds, they get up so early. And Roo was wiser than most cocks, for he was older than most. As Cocorico's special friend, his life was spared till he was too tough for the pot; and after that, he just went on living and living because he was too tough to die.

So Roo gave Cocorico many a farming and weather hint, and Cocorico passed them all on to his father. Over the years, the farmer never once found his son to be wrong. If Cocorico said today would be a good day for winnowing or a bad day for ploughing, however unlikely this seemed at the time, a high wind or storms of rain always blew up later.

Early in one January, when Cocorico had just grown up, Roo told him:

"There will be no barley harvest this year, dear soul."

"Why not, dear soul?" asked Cocorico.

"It is the flame that falls into the seed that makes the barley grow, dear soul," said Roo. "It falls only in the twelve days after Christmas; and this year it has not fallen. It will not fall again till men get busy and renew it."

When Cocorico went indoors to breakfast, he said:

"Father, you will eat no bite of any barley you sow this spring. You will get more good from it if you leave it stored in the grain loft."

Because he had never yet found Cocorico wrong, the farmer sowed no barley that spring. But because he feared he would be laughed at, he told nobody why. When harvest time came round, there was not a handful of barley to be reaped in the whole kingdom. Every grain loft in the land was empty except that of Cocorico's father.

This came to the ears of the king, and he sent for the farmer.

"Dear soul," said the king, "why is your grain loft still full when all others are as bare as my hand?"

"Your Majesty," said the farmer, "because I stored my grain this spring instead of sowing it."

"Why did you do that, dear soul?" asked the king.

"Your Majesty," said the farmer, "because my son told me to."

"Send for your son, dear soul," said the king.

When Cocorico came, the king asked him:

"Dear soul, why did you tell your father not to sow his grain this spring?"

"Your Majesty," said Cocorico, "because I knew it would bear no harvest."

"Why not, dear soul?" asked the king.

"Your Majesty," said Cocorico, "because no flame fell into the seed in the twelve days after Christmas."

The king nodded his head. He knew about seed flame needing to fall. It is a king's business to know such things.

"Will it fall next year, dear soul?" he asked.

"Your Majesty," said Cocorico, "only if men get busy and renew it."

Now the king was very old, and he had no child to rule after him. He had long been seeking for someone to take as his heir, someone who would care for the kingdom as a king should.

"Dear soul," he said now, "I think you may be just the young man I am looking for. Go and get this seed flame renewed, and you shall be heir to my kingdom."

Cocorico went back to the farmyard, and told all this to Roo.

"It will not be easy, but it will not be hard," Roo told him. "The flame comes from Out of This World. All you have to do, dear soul, is to marry a princess from Out of This World, and she will bring back the flame as her dowry."

"Where is Out of This World, dear soul?" asked Cocorico.

"Out of this world, of course, dear soul," said Roo. "You simply go north till you get there. Ask the Cock of the North when you can go no farther."

So Cocorico set out on his journey to Out of This World. North he walked, and north he walked, and still north he walked, till his shoes were in holes, and his stockings, too. He walked for months and months; he walked till nearly Christmas.

All the time it got colder and colder, till at last he came to a land where there was nothing but snow on all four sides of him, and the snow in front of him rose like a wall. And there he met the Cock of the North.

"Am I near to Out of This World, dear soul?" he asked the Cock of the North.

"There is only this wall between you, dear soul," the Cock of the North replied after a moment, flapping his wings to keep warm. "This is the place where, once every twenty-four hours, the Earth turns on its hinges. Wait till you hear them creak, and you can slip through."

Cocorico waited till the Earth turned on its hinges. He heard them creak; he slipped through; he was in Out of This World.

Out of This World was indeed out of this world. He slipped through from grey skies to blue; from the snowfields to cornfields standing tall and golden; from the winds as sharp as a shearing-knife to air as soft as a May morning.

He came to a well, brimming with bright water, and he lay down and drank from it. The water of that well was sweeter than white wine.

As he drank, he heard a girl's voice singing; it seemed to be coming nearer. In a flash Cocorico was on his feet and hidden among the foliage of the tree overhanging the well.

From within his screen of leaves, Cocorico saw first a pair of shapely bare feet pause under the tree, a plain white robe kilted above them. Then he saw the white-clad shoulders and the bound yellow hair of the girl as she knelt at the brink of the well, her hand on her water jar. Before she dipped it, she leaned forward and stared at herself in the calm mirror of the water.

Cocorico bent from among his boughs to stare at her, too. The face he saw in the well was fresh and young and sparkling, with a red poppy behind one ear, and a most bewitching mole at the left corner of a saucy mouth. He thought it the most charming face he had ever seen.

Then, all at once, the smiling eyes widened; the girl's whole form stiffened; and close to her dazzling reflection he saw what she had just seen — his own.

Dark youth, fair girl, they stared at each other in the water without speaking. Then he saw her reflection place a finger on its lips. A moment later and the mirror was shattered into ripples as she dipped her water jar and rose, lifting it to her shoulder.

As she slowly moved away, she started to sing again, softly yet clearly, as if her song were meant for him. And this was what she sang:

"If Coquelicot you would win,
Cock must not crow;
Horn must not blow.
Open the gate, and enter in.

Seek you fresh flame to feed your sheaves?
Do not forget
That never yet
Has holly lost its glossy leaves.

When twenty golden girls you see,
All gleam, all grace,
All fair of face,
Remember me! Remember me!"

Cocorico waited till the song had died away; then down the tree trunk he slid. He plastered down his drakes' tails and cocks' feathers of hair with water from the well, washed his hands and face and pulled up his stockings that were full of holes. Then, squaring his shoulders, he followed the path from the well.

It wandered up a slope of laden peach and pear trees toward a great gate of golden filigree, through which he could see in silhouette a hanging horn, and a warder idly tossing dice as he leaned against it. Beyond rose a stately hall, with walls of silver under a roof of gold.

As Cocorico came nearer, he saw beside the path a golden cock veering to and fro on a tall lookout post. He took it for a gilded weathercock till, as he himself came out from the shelter of the fruit trees, it flapped its wings and stretched its neck and stood on its toes to crow.

"Hist, dear soul!" Cocorico called softly in cock language. "I am Cocorico — you mustn't announce *me*! Help me instead to stop that horn from blowing."

The golden one cocked a shrewd eye at him, then over the golden gate it flew, pounced on the warder's dice in midair and flapped away with the dice. After it dashed the warder, dropping oaths to left and right. Cocorico thrust his hand though the golden filigree, lifted the bar, opened the gate, and walked in.

He unslung the horn, lest the warder should come back and blow it; then, horn in hand, he entered the great glittering hall.

It was empty except for a burly king, asleep on his high seat, his crown on the back of his head. As Cocorico strode up the hall with ringing footsteps, the king awoke and yawned a mighty yawn. Then his gaze fell on Cocorico, and he stared and rubbed his eyes.

"I suppose you have come for one of my daughters, dear soul?" he rumbled.

"Yes, please, Your Majesty," said Cocorico.

118

"Well, dear soul," said the king, "the cock didn't crow and the horn didn't blow, so you're over the first of your hurdles. Now tell me this: will you have her for as long as there are leaves on trees, or for as long as not?"

"As long as not will be winter, when the seed flame falls," thought Cocorico. "Is that the right answer?"

Then he remembered the song of the girl at the well, and instead he answered:

"For as long as there *are* leaves on trees, please, Your Majesty."

"Oh, dear soul!" exclaimed the king in surprise. "You only want her in summer, then?"

"For all the year round, please, Your Majesty," said Cocorico.

> "Do not forget
> That never yet
> Has holly lost its glossy leaves."

"Aha!" chuckled the king, rubbing his hands, well-pleased. "Two hurdles over! Now, *which* daughter, dear soul? It's no use saying you don't mind; you *must* name the one you want."

Again Cocorico remembered the song at the well.

"Coquelicot, please, Your Majesty," he said.

"Coquelicot, eh?" chuckled the king. "Now there's a sly puss for you! Well, dear soul, if you can pick her out, you're welcome to her. That's your fourth hurdle, and your last."

Taking the horn from Cocorico's hand, he blew a loud blast on it. At once the staircase from the bowers above was alive with tripping footsteps and a twittering like an aviary of birds. Then in trooped the princesses, four, eight, ten, twenty of them. They made a ring round Cocorico, took hands, and invited him archly:

"Choose, dear soul!"

Cocorico ran his fingers through his smooth hair, ruffling it into wilder drakes' tails and cocks' feathers than ever. For those twenty princesses were as much alike as a ring of fence stakes (though much more beautiful, of course). And every one of them, he could have sworn, was the girl he had seen at the well.

He looked at them all again. Each had the same piquant face, the same sparkling glance, the same yellow locks, the same graceful form; each gleamed in a long golden dress; each wore a golden star in her golden crown. There simply wasn't a hair to choose between them.

And then he could have jumped sky-high with joy as he remembered that most bewitching mole at the left corner of a saucy mouth!

Again he went round the ring of laughing golden girls till he found that bewitching mole and kissed it soundly; and all Coquelicot's sisters clapped their hands and cried:

"Right, dear soul!"

On Christmas Day, Cocorico and his bride said farewell to the king and her nineteen charming sisters. This time Cocorico did not need to wear his wedding shoes into holes, nor his wedding stockings, either; for the king sent a strong north wind to carry them swiftly home.

All the twelve nights after Christmas, Coquelicot's dowry of seed flames fell thick over all the kingdom; there never *had* been such a barley harvest as the one which followed, even in the long memory of Roo.

As soon as the harvest was safe in the kingdom's

grain lofts, the old king made Cocorico his heir; and in due course he and Coquelicot became king and queen of the land.

Roo helped them to rule it well with his store of farmyard wisdom; in fact, such a tough old bird as Roo is probably helping them still.

The Mirror on the Mountain

On the sixteenth birthday of the King of Spain's daughter, her duenna said to the king:

"Sire, the Infanta is fast growing up. Remember, it is her fate to be brought to you from a mirror on a mountain by the one she is to marry."

"Bless me, is she as old as that already?" exclaimed the king. "I must put on my thinking cap."

And he sent for it from his treasury.

"My men shall find me a mountain," he announced when it was on, "one mile high, one mile wide and one mile long. On its peak they shall build me a crystal castle with ramparts that cannot be climbed. I will set a guard at every crack, and two at every cranny. I will turn a river into a moat. If anyone can bring her to me out of *that* mirror, he *deserves* to marry her!"

No sooner said than done; in no time at all the mountain was found, the river was turned, the castle was built, and the Infanta Esperanta Esterella Isabella was sitting beside the fountain in its rose garden with her duenna.

Now just over the border, in Portugal, a poor widow lived with her son, Torto, and her stepson, Benito. Torto was the apple of her eye; Benito was the dust beneath her feet.

Who had to get up in the dark, to light the fire, and to fetch water from the spring? Who but Benito?

And who, as the sun rose one morning, saw the flashing of a fiery mirror on a distant mountain top? Who but Benito?

Indoors he rushed with the brimming pails.

"Stepmother," he said, "give me food for a journey. I have seen a mirror on a mountain; and to that mirror I must go."

His stepmother ran to the spring, to see the mirror with her own eyes. Back she ran and pulled Torto out of his snug bed.

"Up, lazybones!" she scolded. "Run to the spring and look at the mirror on the mountain. That is where your fortune lies. Be off with you to find it, or Benito will find it first."

She took her husband's fine festival coat from the press for Torto to wear. She filled a knapsack with cake for Torto to eat on the way. She put in a bottle of good red wine of Oporto to quench Torto's wayside thirst.

"Off with you now," she cried, pushing him from the door, "and put your best foot forward!"

But Benito she kept all morning tied to her apron strings. One task after another she found for him to do. And when she could find no more tasks, it was in his shabby out-at-elbows working coat that he had to set out, with only a dry crust in his knapsack, and with an empty bottle which he filled with water from the spring as he went by.

Torto felt very grand as he swung along in his father's fine festival coat.

"All I need now," he said to himself, "is a feather in my cap."

He saw a magpie sitting in a tree, half black as night, half white as day. Up went his hand with a stone in it; *squawk* went the magpie; a black feather fell from her tail as away she flew.

Torto put the feather in his cap, and went whistling on his way. He met nobody but himself till he came to a little old man sitting under an old thorn bush. His head was as bald as a basin, and he wore a leather apron, and spectacles a-tilt on his nose. He was sewing fine snakeskin shoes.

"Sewing leather is hungry work," the little man greeted Torto. "Could a fine young man in a festival coat spare an old shoemaker a crust of bread?"

"No," said Torto curtly. "I have only cake."

And on he swung with his head in the air.

Again Torto met nobody but himself till he came to a little old man sitting on a green knoll. He wore a cocked hat and knee breeches, and silver buckles on his shoes. His cloak flapped in the wind as he strummed on a harp, singing over and over again:

"The sun, the moon, the stars are bright."

"Singing is thirsty work," the little man greeted Torto. "Could a fine young man in a festival coat spare an old harper a drink of water?"

"No," said Torto curtly. "I have only wine."

And on he swung with his head in the air.

When the sun was overhead he came to a wide river. On the other side was a mountain, a mile wide, a mile long, a mile high. A castle of crystal was perched on its topmost crag. Rack his brains as he would, he could think of no way of reaching it.

He sat down under a tree on the riverbank. He ate up all his cake. He drank up all his wine.

"Well, there is the mirror on the mountain," he said to himself. "But as to how to reach it, I am at my wits' end. I may as well have my siesta here, and then go home again."

He stretched himself out in the shade of the tree. In two flicks of a cow's tail he was fast asleep.

As Benito stood up from filling his bottle at the spring, a magpie overhead began to chatter:

"Here's a feather to put in your cap, my boy, a feather to put in your cap."

And she let one of her white wing feathers flutter to his feet.

Benito doffed his cap to the magpie, then set the feather in it.

"A thousand thanks, senorita," he called to her, politely, then went whistling on his way.

He met nobody but himself till he came to the little bald shoemaker sewing fine snakeskin shoes under his old thorn bush.

"Sewing leather is hungry work," the little man greeted him. "Is that a crust I hear rattling in your knapsack?"

"It is," replied Benito, "and half of it is yours."

He sat down beside the old shoemaker, and they munched Benito's crust together.

"Those are fine shoes you are making," said Benito.

"A finer point to my needle," said the old shoemaker, "would make them finer still."

"Let me see it," said Benito.

He ground the blunt point on a rough stone. Before he

could say *Hey presto!* the needle was as sharp as a needle. Before he could say it again, the snakeskin shoes were finished.

"The one who sharpens the needle gets the shoes," said the old shoemaker, slipping them into Benito's knapsack.

"They are far too fine to walk in," said Benito, thanking him.

"They are not meant to walk in" the old man replied, twinkling over the top of his spectacles. "You will find out what they are for when the time comes."

On went Benito. Again he met nobody but himself till he came to the little old harper sitting on his green knoll, his silver buckles winking in the sun, his cloak flapping in the wind as he strummed his harp and sang over and over again:

"The sun, the moon, the stars are bright."

"Singing is thirsty work," the little man greeted him. "Is that a bottle of water I hear rolling in your knapsack?"

"It is," replied Benito, "and half of it is yours."

He sat down beside the old harper and they drank Benito's bottle of water together.

"That was a fine song you were singing," said Benito.

"If one of my strings were not broken," said the old harper, "it would be a finer song yet."

"Let me see it," said Benito.

He took the white magpie feather from his cap, twirled it into a string, and stretched it over the gap. The harper drew his hand across the strings, and the white feather sang with the rest:

"The sun, the moon, the stars are bright;
And brighter still rays forth Earth's light."

"The one who mends the harpstring gets the harp," said the old harper, slipping it into Benito's knapsack.

"But I do not know how to play a harp," said Benito, thanking him.

"You will," the old man replied, eyes and shoe buckles twinkling, "when you are at your wits' end."

On went Benito, till he came to a wide river. He stood on its bank, beside the tree beneath which Torto was sleeping. But he did not see Torto, for he was staring ahead. On the other side was a mountain, a mile wide, a mile long, a mile high. A castle of crystal was perched on its topmost crag. Rack his brains as he would, he could think of no way of reaching it.

"Well, there is my mirror on its mountain," he said to himself. "But as to how to reach it, I am at my wits' end. Didn't the old harper say that was the time to play my harp?"

He took the harp from the knapsack and twanged its white feather string. The harpstring sang:

"He who weds is he who woos.
If to be a prince you choose,
Boy, you have no time to lose.
Quick, put on your snakeskin shoes!"

Quickly Benito kicked off his old peasant shoes, clumsy and thick, with holes in the soles. Quickly he slid his feet into the fine, thin, supple snakeskin ones.

At once he found himself lifted into the air and wafted

129

over the river. He flew as birds fly in fables, swift and sure in their flight; and if the guards taking their siestas in all the castle's cracks and crannies felt his shadow pass over them, they felt it only as the shadow of a bird.

Light as a bird he landed on the castle's crystal battlements, and looked down into a rose garden in the shelter of their walls.

Among the roses, by the cool, tinkling fountain, the Infanta Esperanta Esterella Isabella was taking her siesta; nearby, her duenna was taking hers. One flying leap, and Benito stood beside the sleeping princess.

She was a sight for sore eyes, or indeed for any eyes at all. With her long lashes lying on her cheeks, and her long black hair escaping from beneath her lace mantilla, she looked good enough to eat. Benito felt he could never bear to let her out of his sight again. He stood as still as a stone while he stared, and stared, and stared.

The singing of Benito's harpstring had wakened Torto from his siesta. Lying drowsily beneath his tree, he saw Benito slip on his snakeskin shoes, saw him soar like a bird across the river and up the mountain, skimming the treetops and dwindling till he was a black speck on the crystal battlements.

"Oho!" said Torto to himself. "What one can do, two can do."

Back he ran softly to the green knoll, where the old harper still sat, the cloak flapping in the wind, his silver buckles winking in the sun. He was strumming a new harp and still was singing over and over again:

"The sun, the moon, the stars are bright."

Coming silently behind him, Torto tipped the old harper's cocked hat over his eyes, snatched up the harp, and melted among the trees. He ran softly on to the old thorn bush, where the little old shoemaker still sat, stitching busily now at a pair of bat-skin shoes.

When they were done, he put them on the grass beside him while he yawned, took off his spectacles and carefully rubbed them with a scrap of chamois leather. When he turned to pick up the shoes again, they had vanished into thin air.

Already by then the bat-skin shoes were on Torto's feet. But those feet still stood firm on the ground. Torto plucked at the harp; but the harp was mute. Then he noticed the gap in the strings and saw again in his mind's eye Benito twanging a twisted white feather; so he took the black feather from his own cap, and made a harpstring like it.

As soon as he twanged this harpstring, it too began to sing:

"He who weds is he who woos.
If to be a prince you choose,
Boy, there is not time to lose.
Follow, follow, bat-skin shoes!"

At once Torto found himself lifted into the air and wafted over the river. He flew as birds fly in fables, swift and sure in their flight; and if the guards still taking their siestas in all the castle's cracks and crannies felt his shadow pass over them, they felt it only as the shadow of a bird.

Light as a bird he landed on the castle's crystal battlements, and looked down into the rose garden.

There he saw the Infanta Esperanta Esterella Isabella taking her siesta by the fountain; and there he saw Benito standing as still as a stone beside her while he stared, and stared, and stared.

The Infanta was not really still taking her siesta. The wind of Benito's coming had awakened her; but she lay as if asleep and peeped at him through her lashes, to see what he was like, this stranger she was to marry.

She did not mind his looking poor and being out at the elbows. She looked past all that at his kind eyes, and she hugged herself with joy. For the longer she looked at Benito, the more she saw in him to love.

When she opened her eyes and smiled at him, he thought her as marvellous as a magpie, so black her hair, so white her skin, so black and white her eye.

"I am glad it is you," she told him, "who will take me to my father."

She spoke in a whisper; but her duenna was trained to hear whispers even in her sleep. She woke; and all *she* saw was a peasant boy in rags. *This* was not the bridegroom she had dreamed of for the Infanta!

The scream she gave startled all the guards out of their siestas. Out they rushed, one from every crack, two from every cranny, shouting as they clattered up all the crystal stairways.

As they poured into the rose garden, Torto took a flying leap from the battlements and scooped up the Infanta.

Away went bat-skin shoes, away went Torto in them, away went the Infanta flung across his shoulder, flying as birds fly in fables, swift and sure between the clouds and the treetops.

If Benito had stared too long before, he did not do so

now. Away after them went snakeskin shoes, away went Benito in them, flying as birds fly in fables, swift and sure between the treetops and the clouds.

On they all flew to the north, till, as the sun went down the sky, they left the coast of Spain behind them and began to fly over water. Still they flew north, till, as the full moon came up, they flew over another coast, and a misty land lay below them.

"What country will this be?" Torto wondered to himself.

But the Infanta, who (being a princess) was better at geography, knew it must be Ireland.

Below them they could see lights whirling in rings and spirals. Along the margins of the bogs, the will-o'-the-wisps were dancing with feet as light as egg-shells.

When they saw Torto flying, black against the moon, the will-o'-the-wisps called out:

"Moon and mist and marsh together
Make the merriest dancing weather.
Flying shoes of bat-skin leather,
Dance with us among the heather!"

The call drew the bat-skin shoes down to Earth, and Torto in them, and with Torto the Infanta, flung like a sack over his shoulder. Seeing Benito now black against the moon, the will-o'-the-wisps called again:

"Moon and mist and marsh together
Make the merriest dancing weather.
Flying shoes of snakeskin leather,
Dance with us among the heather!"

Now will-o'-the-wisps have frivolous memories, as harum-scarum as their volatile bodies; and they forgot that ever since St Patrick turned all the snakes out of Ireland, no part of a snake can land on Irish soils. So their call failed to draw the snakeskin shoes, and Benito in them, down to Earth.

But as he passed over them, he swooped; he held out his arms to the Infanta, and she held out hers to him, and away south they flew together in the moonlight and each other's arms till they came at sunrise to the King of Spain's own palace, and a rapturous welcome home.

When Torto would have flown after them, a thousand small hands held him back.

"Dance with us! Dance with us! Torto!" cried the will-o'-the-wisps.

So, willy-nilly, Torto danced with them. They capered about him like bright blobs of quicksilver; but Torto was in a fine temper and danced like a lump of lead.

"Strip off his bat-skin shoes!" the will-o'-the-wisps shrilled, enraged; and a thousand small hands did so.

"Since you cannot dance," said the will-o'-the-wisps, "make music for *us* to dance to."

So, willy-nilly, Torto played his harp. As he sullenly twanged his black feather string, it sang:

"The sun, the moon, the stars are bright;
But Earth remains as black as night."

"He is playing lies!" cried the will-o'-the-wisps. "Take his harp away, and duck him in the bog!"

And in the bog Torto found himself when he woke at dawn; he scrambled out of it with a face as long as two days put together. Bruised and barefoot, he limped his way to the Irish coast, and found a ship short-handed, and worked his passage back to Portugal. So he came home to his mother as poor as he had left her, and with his father's fine festival coat plastered with Irish mud.

But from that day to this he has never again thrown a stone at a magpie. So you see there is still hope for him.

The Four-Leaved Clover

Sappho was one of the queen's milkmaids. Out in all weathers, breathing sweet air, she was as brown as a peatpool, as strong as a heather root, as wholesome as the new milk she brought from meadow to castle each sunrise.

Her way led her past the head of a valley filled from side to side with a forest of red yew trees. One morning, as she tripped by with her pail of milk on her head, she stopped dead in surprise. For, rising above the treetops, she saw spiral stone chimneys where she had never seen chimneys before; and out of the spiral chimneys rose spiral columns of smoke.

"But a house can't spring up overnight, like a mushroom!" Sappho exclaimed.

She lifted the pail from her head as she stood gazing; and the wreath of fresh grass it had rested on slipped from her brow and fell to the ground. At once the chimneys vanished, and the smoke with them.

Sappho picked up her grass garland; back came the chimneys; back came the smoke with them. Down she sat and took the wreath apart. Among the meadow flowers mixed with the meadow grasses, she found a four-leaved clover.

Now a four-leaved clover, as Sappho knew, can make the right kind of eyes see things other eyes just can't see. Not everybody has the right kind of eyes; but Sappho had them.

She took the four-leaved clover home and set it in a pot on her window ledge. Here it took root and grew. And, her tongue being as small as her heart was big, she did not tell a soul what she had seen.

Winter came round. The cows were brought in, to spend it in their stalls. Sappho no longer passed the forest of red yew trees every morning.

But every day now she saw Prince Pepin, the king's only son, ride out to hunt. Every day she would watch him out of sight, then come back to herself with a sigh and only half her heart.

One day Prince Pepin did not come back from hunting. But a letter fell out a wreath of mist into the queen's lap. It demanded the kingdom as the prince's ransom.

"But if, in spite of all my safeguards, you can rescue him," it ended, "you will never again be troubled by *Simeon the Sorcerer*."

Simeon the Sorcerer was a dreaded name in that kingdom. No one knew him; no one had ever seen him; no one knew where he came from; no one knew where he lived. But three years ago he had stolen the queen's luck-bringing black bull calf, Star, whom Sappho had brought up by hand; and since then, nothing in castle or cottage had been safe from him.

Company by company, the king sent out his men to scour the whole kingdom — every city, every hamlet, every hill, every valley, every forest, every plain. But no trace did they find of Simeon the Sorcerer; no trace did they find of Prince Pepin.

Sappho watched them go, watched them return.

"Now I wonder?" said Sappho to Sappho.

Night and snow were falling together as she pinned her four-leaved clover over her heart and set out for the head of the valley. If the chimneys were there, night and the snow-storm blotted them out. She said a small charm; she said a big charm; then into the black, black void of the forest she plunged.

Presently she saw gleams between the yew trees; presently she stood before a vast black mansion, scattered from ground to turrets with lighted arrow-slits. Burst of wild music came to her, bursts of loud laughter and revelry.

She dimly saw that she was in a great, snow-covered courtyard, bounded on the far side by a long, low bulk which her milkmaid's sense knew at once for a cattle byre. From it, in gusts between the gusts of wild music, came sounds she knew — the earth-rending stamp, the bloodcurdling snort, of a bull prepared for battle.

She crossed to the byre door and listened. The bull must be loose — to and fro, to and fro went his stamping from wall to wall. And — could it *really* be that she caught a stifled groan?

She pushed open the door; she felt the bull's hot breath on her. She saw him stand, black and monstrous in the dim light cast by a horn lanthorn, his eyes fixed on her, wicked and red, his battering ram of a head lowered ready to charge.

Then he sniffed, and his rage drowned out of him. He took her hand gently into his mouth, and she felt the rasp of his tongue as it curled, sucking, over her fingers. Just so had rasped the tongue of Star, the queen's black bull calf, when, before he could eat grass, she had dipped her hands in deep pails of whey gruel and let him suck them dry.

She turned the massive, passive head toward the lanthorn. Yes, there was the five-pointed white star on his black brow.

"Star! Star!" she whispered and, fondling his ears, stepped beside him toward the dark corner from which came laboured breathing.

The limp form of a youth stirred painfully at her coming. Passing light hands over him, she found him bound hand and foot, too tightly for her untying. The eyes in the blood-drained face lifted, looked deep into her own, then closed again.

"It is I, Sappho," she murmured. "Lie still, my prince. Leave all to me."

She gathered up the weak form in her strong arms, lifted him, heaved him onto the broad back of the quiescent bull.

"Come, Star!" said Sappho.

And out of the byre and the courtyard, through the night and the whirling snow, she led black bull into black forest.

The sky was sowing snow, the wind was winnowing snow, when, later that night, a blast on the guest horn at the castle gate summoned the warders. No footprints led to the gate; none led from it; the snow had filled them up as soon as they were made. But there at the warders' feet lay the lost prince, unconscious, bound hand and foot, but, praises be, still living.

All over the castle, lights were kindled then; all over the castle, joy was kindled with them. But the queen, watching through the night at her son's bedside, pondered a mystery:

He did not find his own way back alone, bound hand and foot. Someone brought him. But who? And how?"

Next morning news was brought from the royal farm that Star, stolen by Simeon the Sorcerer three years ago, had been found there at dawn, chained in his own byre.

And again the queen thought:

"So Star brought him home. But who among my son's friends would know how to handle a bull, or even know which had been Star's byre three years ago?"

The days passed; but Prince Pepin still lay in his bed, pale, silent, lost and languid. The queen was old enough to know lovesickness when she saw it.

"Where does she live, this lady you love, my son?" she asked.

"Nowhere, Mother," he answered faintly. "I met her in a dream."

Next day, before the king's daily visit to his son, the queen had the legs of the prince's bed sawn through.

"Why do you do that, Mother?" asked Prince Pepin.

"To get you your heart's desire, my son," she told him. "Lie still. Leave all to me."

"Someone else said that to me lately," said Prince Pepin listlessly, "but I cannot remember who."

When the king came in and sat down with a bump on the edge of the bed, as he always did, *crash* it went, king, prince and all.

"My golden garters! What was that?" asked the king, scrambling to his feet and dusting down his royal robes with his royal handkerchief.

"Our son's heart," said the queen. "It is so heavy that the bed broke under him."

"Heavy with what?" asked the king.

"With love of a lady he met in a dream," said the queen.

"Is that so?" said the king, rolling his eyes. "Get better, my son, and you shall marry somebody real."

But Prince Pepin did not get better.

So, a few days later, again just before the king was

due to visit his son, the queen scattered dry crumbs in the prince's bed.

"Why do you do that, Mother?" asked Prince Pepin.

"To get you your heart's desire, my son," she told him. "Lie still. Leave all to me."

"I remember now," said Prince Pepin dreamily. "It was she who said that before she rescued me."

"Who?" asked the queen.

"She told me her name," said the prince, groping in his misty mind, "but I have forgotten it."

"Now I know a little more," thought the queen. "It was a maiden who rescued him."

When the king came in, he sat down with a bump on the edge of the bed, as usual. The prince rolled over, to give him room. *Crack, crack, crack* went the dry crumbs under him.

"My golden garter! What was that?" cried the king, frightened out of his wits.

"Our son's heart," the queen told him, "breaking for love of the maiden who rescued him."

"Then let him marry her," said the king, "before this heart of his pulls down the whole palace about our ears."

"Whoever she is?" asked the queen.

"Whoever she is," said the king. "And who *is* she?"

"Nobody knows," said the queen. "He has forgotten her name."

"Pooh!" said the king. "That is easy. Just make me a list of girls' names, and I shall soon find out."

The queen sat down with a roll of clean parchment before her, and nibbled the tip of her goose feather quill.

"Which of my maidens would be strong enough to lift him?" she asked herself. "Only my milkmaids. Which of my maidens would know about Star? Only my milk-maids."

So she wrote down all her milkmaids' names, and handed the list to the king.

The king put on his gold-rimmed spectacles, and looked over the top of them at the prince each time he read out a name. But the prince lay with his head on his pillow, pale and lost and languid, and did not open his eyes from first to last.

"Your mind does not remember, my son," the queen said then. "Let us see if your heart does."

She laid her fingertips on the prince's wrist and asked the king to read the list again.

She could feel her son's pulse, still slow and faint and languid, as name followed name. Then all at once it gave a mighty leap.

"Stop there, dear," said the queen to the king; and to Prince Pepin: "So it was Sappho, my son?"

"Was it?" Prince Pepin answered, still all lost and languid.

The queen sent for Sappho. As she came shyly into the prince's chamber, he gave her one look and in two shakes he was out of his bed and across the room and holding her tight in his arms.

When Princess Sappho went with her four-leaved clover to find Simeon the Sorcerer's house again, it had vanished into thin air. And, just as it said in his letter, he has never troubled that kingdom again from that day to this.

And though by now we have forgotten why, to this day we still think it lucky to find a four-leaved clover.

The Shining Loaf

The seven royal physicians standing in a row at the sick king's bedside shook their seven heads at the three black moneybags painted on the shield he had had laid over him.

"Not all the moneybags in the kingdom can save your honourable father," they told the small Princess Cordelia. "Mother Grana might; but she disappeared into The Blue when cottage loaves went out."

Cordelia tipped her little gold crown over her left eye to help her to run faster; and away she ran — out of the marble bedchamber, down the marble staircase, out at the wrought iron gates, out of the city, over the moor, to the door in the high wall that held the kingdom together. It was locked, and it was padlocked, but it flew open at her touch; and out she shot into The Blue.

Out of The Blue loomed a rose-red cottage, with birds singing on its thatch of golden straw. In at its open door went Cordelia, into a white, bright, spotless, speckless kitchen, with a fire of wheat-straw burning with clear golden flames on the hearth. The homeliest, comeliest peasant woman Cordelia had ever seen stood at the scrubbed ashwood table, kneading shining dough into shining cottage loaves. She was rather like a shining cottage loaf herself.

"Our bread doesn't shine like that," said Cordelia.

"That is the pity of it," said the peasant woman.

"What makes yours shine?" asked Cordelia.

"The sun in the wheat," said the peasant woman.

"What makes your fire golden?" asked Cordelia.

"The sun in the straw," said the peasant woman.

"Why is that wall around the kingdom?" asked Cordelia.

"To keep people in," said the peasant woman.

"But I got out," said Cordelia.

"Children can," said the peasant woman.

"So did Mother Grana," said Cordelia. "Can you tell me where to find her?"

"You *have* found her," said the peasant woman.

"Quick, Mother Grana!" cried Cordelia then, tugging at the cottage-loaf skirts. "King Moneybags needs you."

They shot out of the cottage and out of The Blue and in at the door in the wall, over the moor and into the city, in at the wrought iron gates, up the marble staircase and into the marble bedchamber.

"Put out your honourable tongue, Your Majesty," said Mother Grana.

King Moneybags put out his honourable tongue.

"Mercy on me!" cried Mother Grana. "Your Majesty's honourable tongue is too foul for words. Only one thing can clean it — three crumbs from a shining loaf that is a free gift from your kingdom."

"Who ever heard of a free gift in *my* kingdom?" demanded King Moneybags. "And who ever saw such a thing as a shining loaf?"

"I did," said Cordelia. "In Mother Grana's cottage, out in The Blue."

"Then I will graciously accept it," said King Moneybags.

"*That* will not clean Your Majesty's honourable tongue," said Mother Grana, "for *that* would not be a free gift from your own kingdom."

Cordelia tipped her crown over her left eye to help her run faster; and away she ran — out of the marble bedchamber, down the marble staircase, out at the wrought iron gates, along the streets of the city, and into a baker's shop.

"Please, Baker, can you bake me a shining loaf?" she asked.

"If you can bring me some shining flour," the baker told her.

Out of the baker's shop she shot, and ran to a mill.

"Please, Miller, can you grind me some shining flour?" she asked.

"If you can bring me some shining grain," the miller told her.

Out of the mill she shot, and ran to a threshing barn.

"Please, Thresher, can you thresh me some shining grain?" she asked.

"If you can bring me a shining sheaf," the thresher told her.

Out of the threshing barn she shot, and ran to a ripe cornfield.

"Please, Reaper, can you reap me a shining sheaf?" she asked.

"If you can sow me some shining seed," the reaper told her.

Out of the harvest field she shot, and across the Bridge of the Seasons into a spring ploughland.

"Please, Sower, can you sow me some shining seed?" she asked.

"If you can fill me a sieve with sunlight to steep my seed in," the sower told her.

Cordelia held the sieve up into the sunlight. Into the sieve streamed the sunlight, and away again out of it.

Then a bird came out of The Blue, and perched on the bough above her, and began to sing:

"Sweet, sweet, sweet, sweet!
My song I give
As a gift, gift, gift, gift, gift!
Plaster your sieve
In each rift, rift, rift, rift, rift!
Light will not leak away
If you caulk it with clay.
Daub it! Daub it! Daub it!"

Cordelia filled all the holes with clay, and the sunlight streamed in and filled the sieve to the brim. Back she ran with it to the sower.

"It was a gift from a bird from The Blue," she told him, as he stood and gaped in amazement.

"Then let the sowing be a gift, too," said the sower.

He steeped his seed in the sieveful of sunlight, and sowed it; and as he sowed, he thought:

"Why do I feel so happy?"

The young corn sprang up and grew green and tall; and ears filled and turned golden, ready for harvest. Cordelia had hardly got back her breath after running before the corn began to shine.

She ran to fetch the reaper, to reap the shining corn.

"It was a gift from the sower and a bird from The Blue," she told him, as he stood and gaped in amazement.

"Then let the reaping be a gift, too," said the reaper.

And as he reaped a shining sheaf, he thought:

"Why do I feel so happy?"

Cordelia ran with the shining sheaf to the threshing barn.

"It was a gift from the reaper, the sower, and a bird from The Blue," she told the thresher, as he stood and gaped in amazement.

"Then let the threshing be a gift, too," said the thresher.

And as he threshed the shining grain and filled a grain-bag with it, he thought:

"Why do I feel so happy?"

Cordelia ran with the shining grain to the mill.

"It was a gift from the thresher, the reaper, the sower, and a bird from The Blue," she told the miller, as he stood and gaped in amazement.

"Then let the milling be a gift, too," said the miller.

And as he ground the shining flour and filled a flour bag with it, he thought:

"Why do I feel so happy?"

Cordelia ran with the shining flour to the baker's shop.

"It was a gift from the miller, the thresher, the reaper, the sower, and a bird from The Blue," she told the baker, as he stood and gaped in amazement.

"Then let the baking be a gift, too," said the baker.

And as he mixed it and kneaded it and shaped it and put it to bake, he thought:

"Why do I feel so happy?"

Cordelia had hardly got back her breath from running when he opened the oven door again and took out the shining loaf.

"Goodness!" he cried. "Just look what shape I have made it! This is the first cottage loaf I have made since cottage loaves went out!"

Cordelia ran with the shining loaf along the streets of the city, in at the wrought iron gates, up the marble staircase and into the marble bedchamber.

She thrust the shining loaf into Mother Grana's hands.

"It was a gift from the baker, the miller, the thresher, the reaper, the sower, and a bird from The Blue," she told her.

"Good," said Mother Grana. "That makes it a free gift from the kingdom. Open your honourable mouth, Your Majesty!" ordered Mother Grana.

King Moneybags put out his honourable tongue.

"As clean as a whistle!" reported Mother Grana.

Outside there sounded a whistle like nothing on earth. Cordelia ran to the window, and she saw that the high wall that ran around the kingdom had disappeared into The Blue, and The Blue came pouring in.

Up rose the king from his bed. He dressed his honourable self in his golden robes and his golden crown.

"Fetch me my palace scrub-woman," he told his seven royal physicians, "and a big pot of gold paint."

When they had done so, he begged the loan of Mother Grana's white starched apron and his palace scrub-woman's scrubbing brush. He rolled up his cloth-of-gold sleeves, and he tipped his crown over his right eye, to give more power to his elbow. Then right off his shield he scrubbed the three black moneybags; and in their place he painted a shining cottage loaf.

King Arthur's Gold

Each sunrise Mia led her father's flock from the fold. They lay busily growing wool all day on a round mound of a hill called King Arthur's Castle, where the turf was close and lush; the sheep they had in those days knew a sweet bite of grass when they saw one.

Each noon Mia sat down by King Arthur's Well; on its brink she spread her handkerchief, as clean and white as whey; and on her handkerchief she laid a ripe red apple and a crust of good black bread.

"Auntie Frog!" she called.

Auntie Frog popped out of her cold bath (she was a great believer in cold baths), and hopped up to share Mia's meal.

While they ate from the handkerchief, while they drank from the well, Mia told Auntie Frog how the fences were falling down, the gates were falling off, the walls were falling out, the roof was falling in; for her father was so poor that he had not a flitter to fly with.

"No matter and never mind, child," Auntie Frog comforted her. "One fine day that farm will be as neat as a new pin."

"Oh, *when*, Auntie Frog?" cried Mia.

"When your sheep turn yellow," said Auntie Frog.

"What could make them do that?" asked Mia.

"Lying on hidden gold," said Auntie Frog.

Mia watched for the curly fleeces to change colour;

and, believe it or not, one day they did. She ran to the well to tell Auntie Frog. She was so excited that she hardly knew which leg to stand on.

"Didn't I tell you so?" said Auntie Frog, blowing herself up big.

"But where is the hidden gold?" Mia asked. "And why is it suddenly where it wasn't?"

"It is King Arthur's gold," Auntie Frog told her. "From deep in the earth it rises a cock's stride every year till it lies in his castle. If you can get in before the gold sinks again, a lapful, a crockful and a kettleful are yours."

"Won't King Arthur mind?" asked Mia.

"Not he," said Auntie Frog. "He knows that those above ground need gold more than those below."

"How can I get in?" asked Mia.

"By the castle door, like a Christian," said Auntie Frog.

"But doesn't King Arthur keep that locked?" asked Mia.

"Of course he does," said Auntie Frog. "Kings *do* when they settle down to sleep for centuries. But do as you would be done by, and you will find the key."

Mia had taken seven steps — she had taken no more, she had taken no less — when she heard the woodpecker nestlings squawking to be fed. She saw them popping their heads from their nest-hole in the hollow tree trunk in frantic search of lunch and father. She heard Father Woodpecker himself tapping a distant tree trunk for grubs with his beak of bone. She saw the slinking stoat, evil and avid, mark down the defenceless nestlings as his prey.

Flinging her crook at him, Mia heaved up a rock with both hands and with it shut the nestlings into safety. But when the stoat had slunk away, and Mia tried to

dislodge the rock, she found it was too firmly wedged in the woodpeckers' doorway.

"No matter and never mind, child," said Father Woodpecker, swooping home with a beakful of delicacies; and with a flourish and flash of green wings, red crest and golden rump, away he flew.

Back he darted with a blue flower in his beak; round the tree trunk he flew nine times against the sun; then he touched the rock with the flower. Out fell the rock; out popped the nestlings all shrill with indignation; down swooped Father Woodpecker to lay the flower in Mia's hand.

Mia ran seven steps — she ran no more, she ran no less — back to King Arthur's Well. Auntie Frog, blowing bubbles, rose out of her bath.

"Didn't I tell you so?" said Auntie Frog, blowing herself up big. "Off with you, child; nine times round King Arthur's Castle with the blue flower in your hand. As soon as you see the door, touch it with the flower, and it will open; wedge it with your crook; and in you will go!"

"And then, Auntie Frog?" gasped Mia, breathing very hard.

"Do not wake King Arthur and his knights," said Auntie Frog. "Tread softly; do not even look at them; do not turn your head or eyes either to left or to right. Let your back be to them, let your face be from them, as you take your lapful and your crockful and your kettleful of gold. Tiptoe out with the gold; pick up your crook; and there you are!"

Nine times round King Arthur's Castle ran Mia against the sun, the blue flower in her hand. All at once, there in the side of the grassy mound, she saw a door, framed in great standing-stones. When she touched it with the flower, the door swung slowly inward, into a passage bathed in a gentle milky light. Wedging the door open with her crook, holding her breath, her heart in her mouth, Mia stepped across the threshold.

In utter silence she moved along the passage, between walls of rock glittering with quartz and feldspar. In utter silence she passed beneath a lofty gateway into a chamber like a church. Its high roof, studded with rock crystals, was supported on massive alabaster pillars, luminous with their own inner light; from carved arches, soaring and crossing in the dusk above, hung lamps like a giant's pearls.

In the shadows beyond their milky radiance, Mia caught a glimpse of sleeping forms in golden casques and glinting armour. She did not look at them; she did not turn head or eyes either to left or to right. She let her back be to them, she let her face be from them, as she gathered a lapful, a crockful and a kettleful of gold. For gold lay as thick upon the black and white chessboard floor as fallen leaves lie in an October beechwood.

Knotting up her smock with its lapful of gold, crock full of gold in one hand, kettle full of gold in the other, without a backward glance she passed, as silent as still air, out of that still chamber, along the silent passage, over the heavy stone threshold; and there she was!

She took up her crook, and the door closed silently between the standing-stones. When she looked again, the turf lay smooth and green, and she could not even see where door or standing-stones had been.

As she went by King Arthur's Well, Auntie Frog popped out of her bath and hopped with marathon leaps to roll her bulging eyes at Mia's glittering burden.

"Didn't I tell you so?" said Auntie Frog, blowing

herself up big. "Drop the blue flower in the well, child, to keep it fresh for other folks who do as they would be done by."

The farm now is spick and span, as bright as a new penny, as neat as a new pin, with a fine fat cow for every day of the year; there is nothing that is of use on a farm that is not to be found on that one.

"Didn't I tell you so?" says Auntie Frog, blowing herself up big.